"Stay With Me by Ruth E. Griffin took me on a serious roller-coaster ride. I was not expecting her to have my emotions gripped from the beginning to the end. Not only entertaining, but heart wrenching. I read this book literally in a day and a half. While the story has its humorous points, Griffin delves into some serious themes which take the story to another level. I was really touched by this book. It's truly unforgettable, since both lead characters leave an impression on the reader. To the author, I say well done!"

-Daria White for Readers' Favorite

Other Books By The Author

After The Call

Full of Grace

Speak Tenderly To Her

Stepmother's Anonymous

The Best Love

The Book of Joy

Ruth E. Griffin

STAY
WITH ME

Studio Griffin
A Publishing Company
www.studiogriffin.net

STAY
WITH ME

To Mo, my "Noah"

Sometimes the heart sees
what is invisible to the eye.
H. Jackson Brown, Jr.

One

THE CHIME ON THE DOOR announced the arrival of a customer to Mister Bill's Used Books. Noah could hear it from the stockroom. He thought nothing of it though and continued unpacking the box in front of him. Mister Bill, or rather just Bill, stocked mostly used books, donated from libraries, customers and other bookstores. Every so though often he would add bestsellers to his collection, not unlike the ones Noah was unpacking today. He didn't know what they were but based on the density and weight of the books, he could tell they weren't a light read.

With the books carefully stacked in his arms, Noah kicked open the swinging door separating him from the rest of the store. He navigated his way through the young adult section into literary fiction where his coworker Jada was flirting with her boyfriend of the week, who was too enamored to even notice Noah. Jada, on the other hand, glanced at him long enough to make sure he wouldn't say anything, then resumed her dalliance.

I'll say something later, he thought to himself, though the truth was, he probably wouldn't.

Noah neared the paranormal romance shelves next. The only thing he knew about this genre was that it was populated with lovesick vampires, forlorn werewolves and gregarious ghosts. He wasn't sure what they had to do with romance, but then there were many things he didn't understand, women being the first.

Though he was in his late-twenties, Noah had had only one girlfriend: Sage. Tall, slender, with blonde-brown hair, she was the epitome of beauty. So, he was a little shocked when she asked him out. She did most of the talking through their first, second and third dates. And most of the kissing too. But then she started making innuendoes about his life, his job and his ambitions, or lack thereof. True, he had been employed at the bookstore since high-school, but he was *employed*. Surely that counted for something. And he had gone from stock boy to manager. He had learned a trade. He could pay his rent and put gas in his car. He wasn't lazy or ambitionless, he was content. Was that so bad?

Apparently for Sage, it was; and after two months of dating, she dropped him in favor of someone with 'bigger' goals—her personal trainer. Noah was devastated, but he found solace in the fact that his life could have been worse. How, he wasn't sure, but things could always be much worse, or so the saying went.

With a resigned sigh, Noah readjusted the bestsellers in his arms and continued forward, turning the corner into the fantasy section, another subject he didn't understand. Yes, he could be pragmatic about things, but to live in a world where reality was set aside for the fantastic? It just didn't make sense. What did dragons, dwarves and leather-clad muscle-heads have on flesh and blood?

His thoughts lost on the subject at hand, Noah didn't notice he wasn't alone in the aisle until he was midway through it. It was only then he glanced up and locked eyes with *her*—a voluptuous beauty with copper-colored tresses that bounced as she walked towards him. She had an almond-shaped face with beautiful brown eyes; full, rosy lips; and the most naturally tanned skin he had ever seen. She had been in the store a couple times before, but each time, Noah was otherwise occupied with Bill or a customer. She was striking then, just as she was now, and as she moved closer to him, he found himself captivated by her beauty. There was something so wondrously intoxicating about her, Noah couldn't help but stare. He stopped walking and simply stood in the aisle, waiting as she drew closer to him. Her steps were soft on the carpet, her feet small and dainty. She was shapely, filling every inch of the shorts and long-sleeve t-shirt she was wearing. Her handbag was tucked underneath her arm, while her hips swayed as she approached him.

You should probably move out of her way, he thought to himself, but his brain had ceased communicating to the rest of his body. He couldn't move.

She stopped, mere inches between them, and gazed at him with her lovely brown eyes. Noah could see the freckles dotting her nose. He could smell the lavender on her skin and in her hair. For a moment, he thought to ask her if she needed help, but he was dumbstruck in that department as well.

Without saying a word, she rose up on her tiptoes and leaned into him. A couple of the books slid out of his arms as she held onto him for support, but she neither apologized nor broke eye contact. She simply smiled, then closed her eyes. She leaned further in, knocking more books out of his arms, and gently kissed him.

Noah's heart was thundering so loud in his chest, he was certain she could hear it. It wasn't every day (or ever) that a beautiful woman walked up to him and kissed him, so once again, he was at a loss of what to do or how to react...until she parted her lips. He felt her tongue on his lower lip and it was all the encouragement he needed. He opened his mouth and let his tongue find hers. The books dropped from his arms, and he intuitively filled them with the mystery woman instead.

As their tongues mated, Noah let his hands slide up and down her arms, feeling the warmth of her body beneath his touch. All thought left him as her hands rested on his chest and her body pressed against his. She felt soft in his embrace—warm, inviting, like she belonged there; and in that moment, she did. Noah was never this spontaneous, impulsive or daring, but something about her just felt right.

The woman took his lower lip in her mouth and gently sucked on it. Then she released him and pulled back ever so slowly, opening her eyes as she went. There was a brief flash of vulnerability in them, followed by a glint of mischief. She dropped her arms and took a step back away from him. Noah suddenly felt empty without her. He was missing something he didn't know existed minutes before; and the worst part was that he still couldn't function—he didn't know what to say or do. It seemed she had robbed him of everything but his breath.

The woman bent down to pick up her handbag, which had spilled its contents on the floor, alongside the books. Instinctively, Noah stooped down with her to help her, but she had already gathered her things. He found himself staring into her eyes instead. She offered him a flirtatious smile then kissed him again, this time quick and playful. She licked her lips, then quickly rose to her feet and started her retreat.

"Noah!" he heard behind him.

Try as he might though, he couldn't pull himself away from the view the mysterious woman was offering him: her lovely backside swinging with every step she took.

"Noah! Noah!"

He gazed over his shoulder briefly to see his coworkers Cass and Jada at the other end of the aisle, wide-eyed and smiling. His face warmed as he imagined what the scene must have looked like to them. Noah turned back to where the woman had been, but she was gone, the door chime announcing her departure as it had her arrival.

"Go after her," Cass exclaimed; and with that command, Noah was seemingly released from whatever trance the woman had him in. With his heart pounding hard once again, he stood up and jumped over the books, running down the aisle towards the door. He didn't know why it didn't occur to him to follow after the woman, but now that he was, he wanted only to catch up to her…though he wasn't sure what he would say once he caught her.

Outside, Noah stopped to look around him. The bookstore was situated in the old downtown area, filled with small shops, restaurants and an urban park. Business was steady enough to keep them all employed, as older adults strolled about, families with little ones went in search of adventure and teenagers loitered…but no woman. Noah ran to the corner and down the cross street, but she wasn't there either.

She was gone.

Disappointed, he returned to the bookstore, his steps slower and heavier. Noah replayed the scene in his head, marveling at the surrealism of it, but also relishing the memory of her kiss. He had always been something of a loner, never finding the time to date (or if he was honest, never finding *a girl* to date). He wasn't especially handsome: dirty brown hair, dull eyes and a lean body. Okay, he was skinny. Skinny and unappealing. So, what was he supposed to make of the woman and her kiss?

The whole thing was just something weird I'll tell my kids about one day, he thought. *If I ever have kids.*

Cass and Jada met him at the door.

"What was that?"

"Who was that?"

"Oh my God, she was gorgeous."

"Did you see her?"

"Damn, she was hot!"

"Who was she?"

"What was that all about?"

"Do you know her?"

"Have you guys dated before? Do you even know each other?"

"I mean, seriously, the way you were sucking each other's faces, right?"

Cass and Jada were twenty-two and nineteen respectively.

Noah shook his head in response—to everything—and continued towards the aisle where he left the books. The women walked with him, Jada's boyfriend not too far behind them.

"Seriously, Noah, who was that?" Cass asked.

"I don't know," he mumbled.

"What's going on?"

The quartet stopped as the bookstore's namesake and their boss, Bill, joined them. He was in his late fifties with a thick midsection and a bald head. He was not a patient man and often talked about closing the store and starting a new business, but he never did. Though he liked Noah, his opinion of young people was very low—they were 'smart-mouthed and mostly lazy' and only lived to aggravate him.

Like today.

"Noah was kissing one of the customers," Jada explained.

Bill glared at him disapprovingly, his eyebrow arched high into his forehead.

"I don't know who she was," Noah argued. He couldn't imagine that fraternizing with potential clients was a fire-able offense, but it didn't hurt to explain himself. "She just came up to me and kissed me."

"They were making out in paranormal romance aisle," Jada added, a broad smile on her face. "Fitting, huh?"

Cass elbowed her, while Noah glowered at his young coworker. Bill seemed to realize then they were not alone. He frowned at Jada's boyfriend and asked, "Who are you?"

Everyone looked to the young man, who shirked back after suddenly becoming the center of attention. He grabbed a book off the shelf and mumbled, "Uhm, I'm here to get a book."

Without a glance in either direction, he wandered off.

Bill said, "Alright girls, back to the front. Noah, clean up," an air of resignation in his voice as though this was something else he should be disappointed with. Then without another word, Bill walked back to his office.

Rather than obey, the young women remained with Noah. As if the questions they had plied him with before weren't enough, Noah knew they were about to unload on him as soon as Bill was out of hearing range. He didn't wait around for the inquisition and moved to do as he was told.

Of course, the girls followed.

"That was kinda romantic, don't you think?" Cass postured out loud, a hint of humor in her voice.

"I don't know," he muttered, wondering at the anonymity of the situation. Then without thinking of the ammunition he would be providing the women, he added, "She's been here a couple times. I've seen her before." He mentally kicked himself when Jada quipped, "Apparently scoping out more than the merchandise."

Noah blushed.

"Well, I think that was romantic," Cass replied, her tone dreamy and lost.

"Why leave then without giving me a name or something? What was that all about?" he asked.

"Aw, Noah's feelings are hurt," Jada mocked, bored with the direction of the conversation. She wasn't always mean-spirited, but she did prefer to be the center of attention.

"Don't listen to her," Cass said, winding her arm in his. Like the mystery woman, she also had a healthy amount of weight on her and stood just inches shorter than him, but they were two different people. Cass was…well, Cass and the mystery woman? There was something about her that had his brain scrambled. "Jada's just jealous," Cass continued, "You have beautiful women stalking you while she has to put out just for a little attention."

Jada stopped walking and placed her hands on her hips, her mouth open in indignation. But when neither Noah nor Cass gave her the attention she wanted, she dropped her arms and ran up beside them.

"Whatever," Jada muttered. "At least I know a guy's name when I screw him."

Noah could offer no objection to that argument.

"Maybe she's playing hard to get," Cass reasoned.

"It would've been nice then if she could've left me a clue or something," Noah said, as they arrived at the books he dropped earlier. He cringed when he saw them: several covers were creased, pages were folded or torn and a couple of spines were bent out of shape. With a sigh, Noah hunched over and started piling up the books, straightening them up as he went along. One-by-one the stack grew, until there was nothing on the floor…except a piece of paper. He retrieved it and looked it over. It was an old receipt with random things scribbled all over it. It wasn't his, nor was it in the aisle before—the woman must have dropped it.

"Seems she did," Cass said.

Two

ALMA CLUTCHED HER HAND-bag tightly and pushed open the door to Mister Bill's Used Bookstore. With her heart pounding in anticipation, she proceeded into the store.

There's nothing to it, she told herself. The plan was simple enough, after all: find Noah, kiss him and leave. What could go wrong?

Everything…just forget this and turn around.

Even as impulsive as Alma was, walking up to a complete stranger and kissing them was not something she did every day. It wasn't something she did…mostly. And it probably wasn't something Noah did ever. But kissing him was something she simply had to do today. He was, after all, the sexiest man she knew.

Well, not *knew,* maybe more like acquainted with; or rather, observed from a distance. Okay, ogled, but it wasn't without deep appreciation for his fine features.

Alma wasn't much of a reader, but on the rare occasion she had wandered into the store looking for a particular book, she saw Noah and knew she had to return. He was thinner than most of the guys she dated in the past, but his angular frame fit him perfectly. He had a head full of dirty brown locks; eyes the color of rich, dark chocolate and a five o'clock shadow that gave him a gruff, yet sexy appearance. She didn't catch his name until her second visit, but by then she knew she had to kiss him.

Inside the bookstore, a young woman was seated on a stool behind the front counter. Alma made brief eye contact with her and quickly wandered into the first aisle she came across. Her steps were quiet on the carpeted floor. She looked around her as she walked, hoping to see Noah. The store was almost empty though, save for another female employee deep in conversation with a young man around the same age. Neither paid her any attention, which was fine with Alma. She didn't need help, she needed Noah.

What if he's got a girlfriend? she pondered as she started up another aisle. Someone as cute as Noah was certain to have a significant other; and with her string of failed relationships, the last thing she wanted was to hear was how he was unavailable. She didn't agree nor did she partake of cheating, but it was better to ask for forgiveness than permission, or so the saying went.

Alma turned the corner, unaware of the genre of books she just passed. That's when she saw him: tall, unassuming, gentle, quiet Noah. He was walking towards her with his arms full of books. His expression was blank, until his eyes met hers. Alma wasn't sure if he even recognized her, but before she could talk herself out of doing what she came to do, she strode right up to him. She stopped long enough to gaze into his eyes, then she leaned in and kissed him.

His lips were soft. She didn't know why that surprised her, but it did, and she liked it. Getting more comfortable with her actions (and the fact that Noah didn't shirk from her in shock), Alma opened her mouth and let her tongue lead her. Noah followed suit. He dropped the books and took her into his arms—another surprise. There wasn't much to him weight-wise, but his embrace was comforting, all-encompassing. Alma would have been happy to stay in it all day…except that wasn't what she came to do. The illicit moment she had sought was already escalating. She had to stop.

Alma slowly pulled away from Noah, who gazed at her with that same blank face he bore just minutes earlier. She considered saying something to him, perhaps thanking him or finding something sarcastic to make light of a situation that was certainly out of the norm, but then she thought better. It was best to leave him while things were still good: he hadn't recoiled in horror.

But that's only because he doesn't know the truth…

And he won't, she told herself. This was all she would get; all she would give.

Only when she was ready to leave did Alma realize she had dropped her purse. She bent down to get it and all her contents. Noah joined her in an attempt to help her. Alma was awestruck—he was like a faithful, little puppy following his master. Unable to help herself, she leaned in and kissed him again, a quick peck on his soft lips, her parting gift. She wanted more, but it was time to go. Alma gave him one last smile, rose to her feet and left.

Item #1 was complete.

"CAN I take your order, Miss?"

Alma looked up at the man behind the counter. She was in line at the coffee shop and it was her turn to order.

"I'd like a white chocolate mocha, please," she replied. It was her favorite drink, regardless of the day and weather. Except today she wanted something different. "Actually," she said, interrupting the barista as he started keying her order into the computer. "Let me get a caramel Frappuccino with extra whipped cream, and extra sprinkles. Please."

"We don't do sprinkles," he said matter-of-factly.

Alma purposely stuck out her lower lip and batted her eye lashes at him.

"Please? I'm celebrating."

He watched her thoughtfully. She widened her eyes and pouted just a little bit more.

"I'll see what I can find," he replied.

She smiled broadly, paid for her drink and moved to the receiving end of the counter. As she waited, she reached into her purse to retrieve her to-do list. Sure, there were apps and fancy do-dads to stay organized, but she preferred the old-fashioned pen-and-paper approach. That way she could see results, as item after item was marked off…like 'Kiss Noah'.

Except the list she made for herself was not in her purse. Alma moved everything around searching for it but came up empty. Panic-stricken, she moved over to a table and rummaged through her bag, pulling out everything so she could see to bottom. Her phone, her wallet, several scrunched up dollars—all haphazardly tossed on the table. Her lipstick and eyeliner rolled close to the edge. Wadded up napkins gracefully fell through the air and landed near her feet. But no list: it was gone.

What did I do with it?

Did she leave it at the apartment? Or on the bus when she rode into downtown that morning? When was the last time she saw it? When did she last physically hold it?

At the bookstore. It was in her hand, mashed up against her purse when she walked in…which could only mean she dropped it when she kissed Noah.

Damn, damn, damn, damn, dammit!

For a split second, Alma considered going back for it. But then it occurred to her she would have to face Noah again if she did that and she wasn't sure she could do it. What if he was put-off by her kiss? He'd had enough time to reconsider his opinion of her. Yes, he was receptive, but then what guy wouldn't be when a beautiful woman such as herself basically threw herself at him? His reaction was scripted by nature, written into his male DNA. Now that he'd had a chance to think things through though, he would have surely reassessed the wisdom of getting involved with someone like her.

Yeah, someone like her.

No, she would just have to go on without it.

A barista called out, "Caramel Frappuccino with extra whipped cream and extra sprinkles."

Alma threw her belongings back into her purse and grabbed her drink. She made it as far as the door and stopped, the smiley, flirty attitude gone. Her heart was pounding, and she could feel a headache coming on. Even her hands were shaking. She was upset and her mood threatened to plummet. She should have been more careful. Yes, the list was insignificant in the grand scheme of things, but it was important for today's purpose.

Pull yourself together, Alma. It's just a stupid list.

Alma took a deep breath and forced herself to stop thinking about it. Today was her day and she was not going to see it ruined because of a piece of paper. Plus, she had other things to tend to, like going to see Rosa. She had told the woman she was coming for a visit and Alma wasn't going to disappoint her.

Taking another deep breath, she composed herself and exited the coffee shop. With quick strides, she walked towards the bus stop, looking for other things to take her mind off the list.

Three

"IT'S JUST SCRIBBLING. NONE of it makes sense," Jada stated as she examined the list. Her boyfriend stood beside her, reading over her shoulder. "Except, of course, for this part about you," she added. Her tone was playful, cheeky.

"Really...," he muttered and snatched the paper from her hand, unappreciative of the attention he was getting. Still, there was no denying it: he was at the top of the list, the mystery woman's intentions plain as day.

Kiss Noah

Part of him swelled up with pride to be ranked so high. But it bothered him that a stranger was making lists that included him. And what about the other stuff?

Talk to Finn

Mail La Vida Book

Extra whipped cream and sprinkles

Sunrise, Sunset

Go see Rosa

Present for Zoey's birthday

Yarn for crochet

Bucket list

Breathe!!!

Get a dog, name it Rick

Pick up paycheck

Die happy

Pick up milk and cereal

Pick up cake and ice cream

Call Leta

New dress

Donations

Do something normal

All the items were scribbled across the page, this way and that, written in different inks, some of it obviously rushed, some of it thought out. It was a list for certain, but it offered no clue as to the woman's identity.

Noah sighed. Everyone present was adamant that he should pursue the matter.

And sure, he'd like to know who she was, but this was an impossible task. He was neither Sherlock Holmes, nor Hercules Poirot. If there was a clue somewhere on the list, then he was missing it.

I guess there's no career as a detective for me, he thought, as Cass joined them. She had been assisting a customer who was looking for a particular book in the romance section—a popular subject today.

"Did you figure it out?" she asked hopeful.

Before Noah could answer, Jada replied, "Nope."

Cass sighed loudly and returned to her place behind the counter.

"Pity. I bet you would have liked to see her again."

Again, before Noah could even open his mouth, it was the boyfriend who spoke up.

"Hell, yeah. That's a sure thing right there, am I right?"

He raised his hand to high-five Noah, but Noah simply glared at him until he dropped his arm. The boyfriend had disappeared for a while after Bill inquired about him, but he was back now, hanging around Jada and interjecting his opinion into the conversation.

"Be nice to Pete," Jada chastised, wrapping her arms around her boyfriend's waist. Pete turned back to Jada and kissed her gently on the lips, apparently grateful for the rescue.

Noah rolled his eyes.

"Besides, if she's such a 'sure thing'," Jada continued, "Why did she leave?"

The question of the hour. But if their silence was any indication, no one had an answer.

"Maybe she changed her mind after kissing Noah," Jada suggested in her usual smarmy tone.

"Jada!" Cass' jaw hung open, offended on his behalf. "Noah's a great kisser. Right, Noah?" She turned to him to respond, but he only blushed.

"And how would you know?" their younger coworker challenged. "You two got something going on in the storeroom?"

"Of course not! I'm just saying. Maybe this chick had other reasons for leaving. Maybe Noah was too much man for her, and she got intimidated."

Noah could feel his face grow hotter.

Jada laughed.

"This is Noah we're talking about! He's not a man, not like Pete. He's like…like…my brother. Eww."

"Well, just because you wouldn't do him, doesn't mean other women don't want to. She obviously did…in the beginning there…"

Noah decided then he'd had enough of the conversation.

"I'm leaving now," he interrupted, turning on his heels.

Cass ran over in front of him and pressed her hands to his chest, stopping him.

"Don't go. Jada will stop being mean."

"Hey, what about you?" Jada insisted, hands on her hips.

Noah took another step towards the storeroom, pushing Cass with him.

"Come on, Noah," she begged. "Let's just try and figure this out, okay?"

As much as Noah hated being the center of attention and the butt of Jada's jokes; and as much as he wanted to extricate himself from the conversation, he desired to know who the mystery woman was more, which meant he was stuck. With a sigh of defeat, Noah did an about-face and returned to his former position, facing Jada and her barrage of smart-ass comments and questions. Cass walked back around the counter and grabbed the list.

"Okay, what do we know for certain?" she asked, perusing the note as the others had already.

"She's a stalker," Jada remarked.

Cass didn't even look up at her coworker,

as she advised, "Jada, if you're not going to help, kindly extricate yourself from the conversation."

Jada rolled her eyes.

"Now we should start with the obvious. Maybe we missed something," Cass continued. "Let's see, she's Latina. Pretty."

Very pretty, thought Noah.

"She's old," Jada said.

Both Noah and Cass gave her a sharp glance.

"I mean, she's old-*er*," she clarified. Then with a shrug of her shoulders, added, mostly to herself, "Well, older than me."

"Okay, then...," Cass said and paused, trying to come up with another detail…

Apparently even the obvious was not so obvious.

"She's overweight," Jada suggested.

"What does that have to do with anything?" Cass retorted, obviously offended.

"I thought you wanted the obvious. She's overweight, isn't that obvious?"

"To who? You? Just because you're a size four? That doesn't make her any less pretty."

"I never said she wasn't. I was just pointing out what was..."

"Yeah, obvious, I get it. I always knew you were shallow, I just never figured..."

"Don't turn this round on me. I won't be disrespected just because I'm honest and tell it like it is..."

"You just use that as an excuse to be mean and put people down."

Jada gasped and Cass exuded attitude. Noah couldn't understand how they had arrived at this point, but he had a sudden urge to flee. And he might have, had Bill not appeared as he did earlier.

"What's going on? Doesn't anyone work here anymore?"

The women looked away from each other, tight-lipped and upset, which left Noah and Pete to answer for them. Or maybe just Pete.

"Seriously, who are you?" Bill asked him, clearly exasperated. "Don't you have a job? Or a life?" He paused and turned his attention back to Cass and Jada. "I'm running a business here, something all of you seem to have forgotten. Now stop the bickering and get back to work!"

No one said anything else. Bill seemed satisfied that the arguing was done and turned around to leave, but not before he addressed Pete one last time: "And get out from behind there. You don't work here."

With Bill gone, silence encompassed their little group. Silence but also fury as Cass and Jada stared each other down. Neither was willing to concede defeat. Noah didn't care either way who won the fight—the purpose of the gathering had been lost in the aftermath. Not that there was even a shot of him finding out who his mystery woman was; with their ranks divided, the task had become impossible.

Oh well. At least she had given him a moment he wouldn't forget.

Leaving the list on the counter, Noah turned around, already focused on the storeroom. There were books to sort through and boxes to pack up. Bill accepted donations from anyone, but not all materials were shelf-worthy and the ones that weren't usually went to thrift stores and other nonprofits. The work wasn't very glamorous, but it was a job.

"She had a tattoo."

Pete's voice stopped him in his tracks.

"I didn't see a tattoo," Noah said cautiously as he turned back.

"That's because you were too busy sucking on her face," Jada said.

Cass narrowed her eyes and gave her a hard look.

"Alright, sorry," Jada told Noah, throwing her hands up. "But you were. That's probably why you didn't see it."

"Where was it?" he asked suddenly hopeful.

"On her neck," she said, indicating the spot. "Her hair got pushed back when you two were suck… I mean kissing. It was a hummingbird, I think." Jada again pointed to where it was. "There was a floral design, really intricate. It looked like it wrapped her shoulder maybe."

Noah couldn't believe he had missed all that. He could picture her face, her hair and her body, but the details surrounding everything else were fuzzy. Still, this was information he could use.

"What?" asked Jada.

"If she got the tattoo here, one of the artists will know her," he said.

Cass clapped her hands and smiled.

"Ooh, so we're going to keep looking for her then?"

"Do you know how many tattoo parlors there are?" Jada asked soberly.

The four looked at each other, no answer to give. Surely, there couldn't be that many.

Jada pulled her phone from her back pocket and opened an internet browser. She did a quick search and seconds later, a list appeared…a rather long list. For a moment, Noah was discouraged. Then Cass, ever the optimist, suggested, "Let's split it up and start calling. What do you say, Noah?"

Noah pondered the situation. He was

supposed to be working and leading by example; he was the store manager, after all. He should be doing right and not chasing after a woman he didn't know. She could be certifiably crazy, psychotic even. At the very least, she was impulsive, impetuous, maybe even rash. Someone like that could be trouble. However, when he recalled the way she felt in his arms, the warmth of her body connecting with his, he knew he had to find her.

"Alright, let's do this."

Four

ROSA HAS ALWAYS BEEN KNOWN for her temperament. As a young woman, others said she had a fiery passion that drove her to live in the moment. Now as an old woman, those same folks just called her a fiery bitch, living in moments past. For Alma, Rosa was just…Rosa. The woman had helped raise her. Alma's *abuela* had assumed guardianship of Alma and her sister Leta when their mother passed away; and because she worked to support the three of them, Rosa, her neighbor at the time, was enlisted to watch the girls after school. Leta was always a good girl, but Alma rejected the thought of conforming to someone else's rules and ideals. This landed her in constant trouble with school in particular, for which Rosa was called upon to bail her out. Alma learned quickly the woman was not to be played with. She could be sweet and loving, but she would not put up with any criminal behavior; and after several whippings at the hands of her demure caretaker, Alma stopped acting out (at school, at least).

The woman continued to watch after her, especially after Alma's *abuela's* passed years earlier. Alma viewed her as the only family she had left (aside from Leta) and after Rosa was placed in a nursing home when she could no longer live on her own, Alma visited as often as possible, keeping her up-to-date on their little family. Today, though, was special. Rosa was going to have *La Vida* book for her.

The bus stop was a couple of blocks from the home. Alma took the time to ready herself for the visit. She loved spending time with the older woman, but she hated the facility. It reminded her too much of hospitals and sickness and all the things she didn't like.

When she arrived, Alma took a deep breath, slipped through the sliding doors and approached the front desk.

"Hey gorgeous," she said, playfully leaning towards Eric, an older, male nurse sitting there. He peered up at her from behind his reading glasses.

"Well, hey yourself," he returned, "Been a while since we've seen you."

She shrugged her shoulders.

"Busy. You know how it is."

"Different kind of busy, but yeah," he said, turning his attention back to the computer. "You're just in time: the witch was just sponged down."

Rosa didn't like the home either and often acted out. Alma knew she shouldn't encourage this type of behavior, but the truth was she was proud of the old woman.

"Oh, she only bit you once Eric. It's not like she drew blood or anything."

The nurse sneered at her.

"There's always next time, right?" he returned sarcastically.

"That's the spirit."

He rolled his eyes then nodded towards the hallway on the right. "Well, she didn't melt, but she should be subdued enough to see you."

Alma knew, despite his grumpy exterior, he really did care for Rosa. So she leaned over the desk and kissed his cheek in gratitude. Then with a turn that would have made her grade-school dance teacher proud, she spun around and headed in the appropriate direction. She skipped down the hall, her mood light again.

"Knock, knock," she said as she entered the room Rosa called her own.

"*Pendejo! Ven aqui, hijo de—*"

The older woman was reclining in her bed on the far side of the room, her arm prepped to throw a water bottle at Alma. The younger woman stopped and raised her arms.

"Whoa, it's me, Alma."

Rosa squinted hard at her. Alma smiled, waiting for the moment of recognition so the other woman could abandon her attack. It didn't take long this time; and with a sigh of defeat, Rosa tossed the bottle on the bed.

"*Lo siento, mija*, I thought it was that nurse."

Alma approached her bedside. Brushing back the stray silver hairs that fell onto Rosa's face, Alma recalled a much younger woman, with hair so black it was almost blue. She always kept it long and found fashionable ways of styling it. She also had the most beautiful pins and barrettes to hold her mane up. Alma got into trouble more than a few times for 'borrowing' them.

"You really should be nice to them, Rosa."

"I'm paying them, so I'm going to treat them the way they treat me."

"They care for you. They treat you good."

Rosa didn't respond, only 'humphed' and turned her face to the television. Alma let the subject drop—there was no changing Rosa's mind once it was set.

"Has Leta been by to see you?" Alma asked, taking a seat next to the bed. Her sister was the more responsible of the two of them, but she didn't make it out to see Rosa that often, citing that she had her own life to live. Alma knew better.

Rosa's response was the same as her last one: "Humph!"

Alma might have chuckled if it was anyone else. But knowing how much Rosa loved her and her sister, and how lonely Rosa got at times, Alma held her tongue and watched the television.

"Leta is too good for her family now. She forgot where she came from," Rosa snarled. "And now she's going to raise that child without even knowing about her family."

Alma listened as the old woman continued.

"I'm not dead yet; I've got half a mind to march to her house and show her and that husband of hers just what it is exactly she's hiding. *Bufón*. And what are you smiling at?"

She couldn't help the smile that crept on her face as she pictured Rosa doing exactly that.

"*Nada, Señora.*"

Rosa fussed for another minute before she changed tune and asked, "How old is her little girl now?"

"Eight. Her birthday is on Saturday," Alma replied and watched as disappointment etched itself into Rosa's face. *If only Leta could see her now,* she thought, *she would visit her more often.*

"Will they have a big party for her?"

Alma turned back to the television. She hadn't been invited, she didn't know.

"Pretty big. You know Leta."

"I'm glad. Children need to be celebrated. And you, *mija*, how are you?"

"I'm fine, Rosa. You know me."

"Yes, I do. That's why I'm asking. Are you staying out of trouble?"

Alma laughed.

"I'm not a kid anymore."

"Well, are you?" Rosa insisted, her tone motherly. She was ready to correct Alma if need be.

"*Si, señora.*"

"Why are you wearing long sleeves? It's supposed to be warm outside today." Rosa eyed her suspiciously. Alma instinctively touched the cuffs of her sleeves and pulled them down. Yes, it was warm, but the older woman did not approve of her tattoos, and Alma had new ones Rosa hadn't seen.

"I'm cold," she lied.

"You have more marks?"

"No. I'm…anemic." At least, she had been last time she went to the doctor. "I get cold easily."

"Are you eating? You look like you lost weight."

Alma laughed.

"Really? Because I still can't get these

hips into those pants you gave me before you moved in here."

Rosa glared at her, as if trying to decide if Alma was telling the truth. But she must have determined it wasn't worth arguing, because she asked instead, "How is your job? You still working?"

"*Si,*" Alma lied, again.

"Good, good," the woman said. "I worry about you, *chiquita*. You act tough but you were always so tender inside."

Alma squirmed in her seat, uncomfortable with where the conversation was going. She didn't mind when Rosa reminisced; memories were all she had left. But not today. This was Alma's day and she wanted to remain positive. She didn't want to think about her shortcomings or about how she failed her family, especially Rosa.

"So, did you get a chance to organize the photos?" Alma asked, changing the subject.

Rosa's face lit up. She threw her arms up and reached over to the shelf on the other side of the bed, where she picked up a medium-sized box. Rosa laid it on the bed in front of her, carefully lifting the lid off. Inside was a beautiful book, with a suede cover decorated with fabric flowers and a die-cut hummingbird and parchment sheets. On the cover was etched the words, *La Vida*, or The

Life. Alma had found it in an antique store and knew it would be perfect for the family photos Rosa had. They were among the few things she kept when she moved into the home and had always expressed interest in passing them onto Leta or Alma. The time and opportunity had come for Alma to take them, but she asked the old woman to organize them first.

"I had forgotten about half of these *fotos*," Rosa commented as she carefully opened the book. Alma leaned into the bed to get a closer look. "Your mother, God bless her, loved to take pictures of her girls."

On the first page was a picture of a beautiful, young Latina with two small girls on her lap. The woman had her arms lovingly around the girls, who looked up adoringly at their mother. Alma didn't remember taking the photo, but she did recognize her mom. And Leta, who was just a few years older than her. They were her world at the time, her everything; and while there was a time when Alma would have cried or gotten agitated just looking at the picture, today it represented a time when things were simpler, and anything was possible.

"She was a beautiful woman," Rosa commented ruefully.

"Yes, she was," Alma agreed as she

reached over and turned the page. Pictures of her mother filled the parchment. She was shapely and attractive, with a head full of straight black hair. Her skin was tanned and flawless. And her smile…Alma tried to remember that smile on her mother's face, but she couldn't. It was always something she had to revert to photos to recall.

Rosa changed the page this time, revealing images of Leta—pig-tailed, crooked-toothed Leta. Alma laughed, knowing her sister would be horrified to see the pictures, despite the fact that she had out-grown all the juvenile things and matured into a beautiful woman who had given birth to a child who was every bit her likeness.

More images followed—of Alma, of the three of them, of *Abuela*, of Rosa. Glaringly absent was Alma's father. But then she had been the result of a one-night stand, something *Abuela* never spoke of. Alma never knew anything about him.

Page after page brought back memories, most of them good, when Alma's mother would spoil them, take them out of school, accompany them on day trips—anything to spend time together. They were wonderful times followed by not-so-good ones. Images of her mother stopped about two quarters of the way through, signaling her death. After that, *Abuela* took custody and Rosa stepped in to help. Times changed, but didn't they always?

"It reads like a story, doesn't it?" Rosa asked as she closed the book. "Your mother would be proud of you girls. *Tu abuela tambien.* Your grandmother too."

Alma nodded her head, surprised with the contentment that filled her heart. The trip down memory lane should have triggered some kind of negative action or emotion, but it didn't. Could it be she was done grieving?

Perhaps it was simply the satisfaction of knowing the next task was fulfilled…

"It's beautiful, Rosa," she said, leaning back towards the bed. She turned and kissed the old woman on the temple, then rested her head on her shoulder.

Five

NOAH SLOWLY EDGED HIS CAR into the parking spot and placed it in neutral, uncertain he actually wanted to stop long enough to get out. He was on a side of town that was usually featured on the nightly news and not for its community outreach. To say he might be putting his life in danger by being there was an understatement. Still, if he wanted to learn the mystery woman's identity, he didn't have much choice.

After an hour of cold-calling tattoo shops, Cass was the one who made the first connection. She spoke with an artist who could identify the hummingbird tattoo. But the man was understandably wary about giving out any additional information.

"Well, you just have to go see him and plead your case," Cass stated, matter-of-factly, after she hung up the phone.

Noah grimaced. He didn't particularly relish the idea of walking up to a complete stranger and requesting personal information on *another* stranger. If anything, he was the stranger of the group and there was no reason he should think that someone would share anything with him.

"Don't be such a wuss," Jada said in her usual brunt manner. "We've come this far. You just gonna give up?"

"Maybe," he replied, more desperately than truthfully.

"Look here, bruh," Pete said and walked over to him. Noah arched an eyebrow as the young man placed a hand on his shoulder and steered him away from the women. "I know you're the sensitive, quiet type, whatever you want to call it, but you need to seriously consider this."

The eyebrow moved higher.

"What's this to you?"

Pete looked over his shoulder, as if to ensure Jada was out of hearing range, then he replied, "Every guy out there dreams of living what you've experienced—having some beautiful broad just walk up to them and kiss them. And granted she wasn't my type, but hey if you're into that kind of bitch, more power to you. All I'm saying is you are living my dream and for my sake…no, for the sake of all mankind, you have to do this."

Noah would have happily punched Pete in the face for his derogatory term for females, but he was too amused by the conversation and the idea that he was somehow the spokesman for mankind. He wouldn't deny that he had dreamed of kissing a beautiful stranger, but now that he was on the other side of that experience, he was still trying to decide what he was feeling.

"What'd you say, man?"

What could Noah say?

No.

But he didn't. Noah rarely said no, even when it was in his best interest and he wasn't yet convinced this was. Especially now that he was sitting outside the tattoo shop. As his car idled, Noah wondered once again if this woman was worth all the trouble he was going to. Then he remembered the touch of her lips on his and the argument became moot. He'd figure out what to say if and when he made it inside the shop.

Before he could change his mind again, Noah turned his car off. He pulled the key out of the ignition and stepped out, locking the door. Not that it would stop any unwanted thieves. Really, as he looked around at the dirty street, littered with trash and graffiti marking the local businesses as gang properties, Noah knew he stuck out in his khaki shorts and lime green shirt prominently displaying Mister Bill's Bookstore logo across the back. It might as well have been a bull's-eye. He had taken off the apron he usually wore at the bookstore, thinking it would help him blend in. Sadly, he was sorely out of place and everyone around him knew it.

Everyone.

Noah proceeded to the front door, sweat beading on his brow. He reached for the knob, but it opened before he could even touch it. Two burly men clad in black leather and sporting beards down their chests pushed past him. Noah shrunk back as much as he could as they grunted and eyed him disapprovingly. He looked away, seemingly studying the 'No Trespassing' sign between them. He could hear shouts and snickering coming from inside the store.

This is a very bad idea, he told himself as the men walked over to their bikes, which were parked in the adjacent alley. The door shut again, and Noah considered leaving, but then another man, wearing low-hanging pants and a bandana (but no shirt) walked up to him. His dark, bronze skin was covered in tattoos and if this wasn't menacing enough, the cigarette that was stuck to his lower lip gave him an extra intimidating appearance. He looked directly at Noah, seemingly wanting something. Noah was too afraid to ask, especially when the man pulled the cigarette from his mouth and blew smoke into Noah's face. Noah grimaced, then coughed. He was going to die.

The man grumbled, as though his

patience was wearing thin.

"My man, you coming or going?" he asked. With a nod of his head, he gestured towards the right and only then did Noah realize he was blocking the entrance. With a sheepish smile, Noah stepped to the left and allowed the man to pass. The door opened to rowdy and hearty laughter as the folks inside immediately recognized the man.

Noah felt like an ass. If he was going to die, it would be by some freak accident in the bookstore, not by the stranger's hand on this side of town (probably). He needed to stop jumping to judgmental conclusions.

Noah took a deep breath, and salvaging whatever dignity he still possessed, he pushed open the door. One step in, though, and he was filled with regret. All eyes turned to him as the ambiance turned awkward. The man who preceded him stood at the counter, glaring at him with distrust. Several others sat in the lobby, like old men in a barbershop. Covered in tattoos, black leather and dirty bandanas, each of them bore a hole into Noah with their gazes and twisted grunts. Another man, who looked like a reject from a punk video, emerged from behind the curtain on the other side of the counter. His hair was purple, he had metal in his ears and lips and his earlobes had been stretched out until they hung on his shoulders.

Noah wasn't racist or discriminatory or anything but...

Yeah, and you know what they say about people who say that...

Okay, so we'll say I'm a coward instead. Better?

Noah let the door slip through his fingers. It shut quietly, hitting his heels and pushing him in. He swallowed hard. He thought to open his mouth and ask to speak to the owner, but his brain had stopped working.

What was wrong with him today?

"Hey, Glen," one of the men in the lobby yelled, sparing Noah from any further indignity, "When'd you'd get a doorman?"

Or not...

Laughter erupted again and everyone went back to what they were doing before. Noah stole towards the counter, where the man with purple hair assisted the one with a cigarette. He didn't dare stare; instead he gazed down at his sneakers, taking interest in the dirt spots covering them. They were once white, true, but constant use had them looking tan and worn. Not that this was important in any form or fashion. His shoes were comfortable and interesting enough to garner his attention until he could speak with the owner.

He really needed to clean them though.

"You lost, buddy?"

Noah looked up. The man with the purple hair was speaking to him. The other guy had disappeared. Noah stepped up to the counter.

"Um, my coworker called earlier?" He paused, waiting for recognition from the man. He got none though. "We called about a hummingbird tattoo...?"

Again, nothing.

"Maybe I can speak ... with ... whomever she talked to earlier...?"

The man continued glaring at him. Noah grew uncomfortable. He tried to think of something clever to add but he found himself as a loss for words again. Maybe this was a sign for him to give up. He had gotten further than he normally would have. He had tried and that counted for something…right?

Noah was ready to leave when the man behind the counter, still glaring at him, yelled, "Glen!"

The conversations around him continued. Obviously, none of them were Glen. The plum-haired man yelled for him again.

"What!" a voice boomed from behind the curtain. Noah swallowed hard as a very tall man stepped through and joined the man at the counter. He had to be about seven feet tall—a full foot and some inches taller than Noah. He was as dark as midnight with a broad, muscular chest and heavily tattooed arms that were busting out of the vest he was wearing.

Because what's the point of getting tattoos if you can't show them off and scare the hell out of everyone, Noah thought.

"This is the guy who called about Alma," the other man said.

Noah wanted very much to deny he said or wanted anything, taking a step or two back as Glen crossed his arms over his chest and stepped forward.

"What do you want with Alma?" he asked. Or rather, growled.

"I...I don't...I don't know who that is," Noah stuttered. Then it occurred to him—they were talking about the woman. "Oh, I mean..." And that was it. No more words. Because he was an idiot and he didn't know how to talk coherently and...well, at least he knew her name now.

Glen shook his head and sighed.

"What'd she do?"

The conversation around them slowly stopped. Noah glanced over his shoulder at his audience and saw expectant, humored faces, waiting to laugh at him once again. He turned back around and glanced up at Glen, who was also waiting on him. But more likely to kill him. For sure this time.

"I…uh…"

Glen raised an eyebrow, waiting…

"I…"

"She must have stole his tongue," someone joked.

"Or his backbone."

Laughter filled the air. Glen nodded to the right and stepped away from the counter. Noah assumed he meant for him to follow. And given the reception he was getting in the waiting room, Noah was happy to go. But not too happy. Especially when they walked into a small room, outfitted with a tattoo chair, a stool and a small table with various needles, inks and a utility knife. Glen held his arm out to the chair and Noah reluctantly sat.

"Now," Glen said, as he dropped into the stool, "What did she do?"

"Uh," Noah began again, eying the man as he picked up the knife off the table. "She, uh…kissed me."

Both of Glen's eyebrows shot up.

"And that's it?"

Noah nodded. Glen placed the knife back on the table and stood up.

"Then consider yourself a lucky man and move on."

He turned to leave.

Noah frowned.

"Wait, what?"

Glen looked back at him. Noah wasn't quite sure if he should be scared anymore or not, still he shrunk back in the chair.

"Leave the girl alone," Glen repeated. "She's trouble."

His tone actually sounded sympathetic, giving Noah some courage.

"Why do you say that?"

Glen looked him up and down. He crossed his massive arms again and leaned against the doorframe.

"She's not the type of girl someone like *you* needs to be tangled up with."

This time, Noah was the one who laughed. A short guffaw, really, because he realized too late he did it out loud. Glen cocked his head to the side, curiously.

"Someone...I mean...someone like me?" Noah said weakly.

"White. Sheltered. Scared. Entitled. Any of these ringing a bell?" Glen asked.

Noah thought to argue—but he didn't dare.

"Look, I'll give you props for coming in here, but Alma is just not the type you mess with." The sincerity in Glen's tone was unmistakable. Noah eyed him, wishing the answers to his questions would simply manifest themselves on the man's face. Of course, none did, so Noah swallowed the remainder of his fears and asked, "You messed with her?"

This wasn't the question he wanted to ask. Well it was, but not like that. He cringed, waiting Glen to pummel him, but the man did not. He sat back on the stool and thoughtfully stared at him. And glared. And gaped. But he didn't respond. Not to that question.

Guess that one was out.

"So…you did her tattoos?"

Glen nodded.

"Hummingbird and flowers?"

Glen nodded again.

"I didn't see them, but I was told it was good work."

"What's your name?" the man asked, changing the subject.

"Noah."

"Noah, I gave you my advice. Alma is a nice girl, but she's not worth your trouble."

He stood up and moved towards the door, ready to leave with Noah's answers. Forgetting his doubts, Noah stood and reached out to Glen. He grabbed the man's arm and pulled. It was like trying to hold onto a tree trunk. Glen stopped and turned back to him.

"Look, I appreciate your advice." Noah released his grip. "But I just need to find out why she did what she did. She came out of the blue and kissed me. At work. In front of my coworkers. And then she left. I... just want to know why, okay? Honestly, I don't know what I'll do if she says she likes me or something like that, I just want to settle this. Can you understand that?"

Glen chuckled, then said, "You know, the last man who grabbed me like that landed in the hospital for three days."

"Oh...," Noah mumbled, though he sounded more like a deflating balloon.

Glen only laughed again. "But yeah, I can understand. I haven't seen Alma in a few weeks though. She works over at the supermarket on Third Street. And you can tell her I told you where to find her. But when it's all said and done, don't say you weren't warned."

Six

"**S**O, WHAT DO YOU HAVE planned for the rest of the day, *mija*?"

Alma shrugged, as she lounged back in the chair beside Rosa's bed.

"Just running errands."

"You have the day off from work?"

Yeah, today and forever…

"No, I'm going in after I leave here. I just had to make sure I visited with my *abuela favorita* first," she teased. Alma's grandmother had always been strict with her and Leta about being respectful towards adults, calling them *Señor* and *Señora*, even *Tio* and *Tia* if it was warranted and they were close enough to the family. Rosa, though, was just Rosa. Because she had never had children of her own, no one ever called her mother or grandmother…except Alma, who was quickly chastised.

"Bah, I'm not your grandmother, a bad kid like you," Rosa, said, batting at the air. It was the same answer she always gave Alma, who promptly laughed.

They visited for a few more minutes before Alma hugged and kissed Rosa. She stopped by the front desk to say goodbye to

Eric, then walked over to the bus stop, feeling happy and light. She couldn't say every visit went like this, but she was glad today ended so well. And she had the photo album *La Vida,* the book of life, her life, Leta's life. Rosa was right: it read like a story. Alma just hoped Leta would like it and show it to Zoey so she would know her family—even if only in pictures.

It had been over a year since she last saw Zoey…at Leta's request. Alma kept in contact with her sister, but their relationship was strained. And as much as Alma wanted to see Zoey and pretend everything was normal, she couldn't. So, she abided by her older sister's wishes and kept her distance, though it killed her to do it.

The bus pulled up to the stop and waited as she boarded. Alma paid her fare and sat down in the first available seat. She smiled politely at the woman across the aisle, then turned her face to the window, still content. She wished she had her list so she could cross off the items accomplished.

After forty minutes and one bus transfer, Alma arrived at the supermarket. She had quit her job the week prior and was only there to pick up her last paycheck. Of course, if she had mentioned that to Rosa, the old woman would have fussed at Alma the remainder of their time together. She might have pulled out her *chancla* too, if she felt it necessary.

"Change your mind?"

Alma was greeted by Mona, one of her former coworkers who manned the customer service desk.

"Nope. Just came back for my last paycheck."

A middle-aged woman with greying hair, Mona removed her glasses and glared at Alma, hands on her hips.

"Yeah, well I'm not supposed to give it to you before Stan gets here. Seems he has some words he wants to share with you."

"Not happening." Alma walked around the desk and joined Mona on the other side. She had been a cashier in her time there, but Alma was smart enough to make friends with the management staff. Well, everyone except Stan. "I need to mail something too. Can you just take the postage out when you cash the check?"

"You want me to lose my job?"

"You won't lose your job," Alma assured her, as she grabbed a large envelope. She reached across the desk and picked up a permanent marker, pushing Mona out of the way. "Stan's incompetent. This store would close without you."

"This is true," Mona conceded, as she

leaned back against the counter behind them, allowing Alma space to finish what she was doing. "That doesn't mean he won't yell at me before I have to remind him he's screwed without me. You've got about five, maybe ten minutes before he gets back. He ran to the bank to make a deposit."

Alma nodded, as she addressed the envelope to Leta. "Then it'll be about fifteen minutes. You know he can't walk by the juice place without getting a smoothie." She inserted the album into the envelope as the phone rang. While Mona answered it, Alma set her purse on the counter and rummaged through it, looking for the other item she intended to mail. Just then, a young woman walked up to the desk. Alma said nothing, assuming Mona would help her. But when she saw the older woman was focused on the phone call, Alma spoke up.

"What's up?" she asked the young woman.

Customer service was not her forte.

"I need to cash a money order."

Alma looked back to Mona, who was still on the phone. She really wanted to make the woman wait so she could finish up before Stan got back, but who knew how long Mona would be on the phone?

"Sure," she said, pushing her purse aside.

The woman handed her the money order. Alma noticed she had a small child with her, a girl, her tiny arms wrapped around her mother's legs.

"Hey gorgeous," Alma said with a big smile.

The little girl hid behind her mother.

"Say hi, sweetie," the woman coaxed, but the girl wouldn't look at her.

Alma took the money order and turned it over, to make sure it was signed. She flipped it back and looked at the amount. Thirty dollars. Okay. She could do this…except she was never trained in the check cashing process. Mona would have to do this. But that would require time she didn't have. Maybe she could give the woman money and cash the money order later. For that, Alma knew she needed the manager's key to open the money till. She looked around the desk.

"Sorry, gotta find the key."

Alma moved papers and looked under folders. She checked on the tack board behind her and in the drawers beneath the counter. She sighed in frustration when nothing turned up.

Just tell her to come back, Alma thought to herself.

Can she shop without it though? A little voice countered.

Honestly, Alma couldn't tell. The woman was dressed well enough—shorts, a t-shirt, sandals—and the child looked fairly healthy. Dirty, but what child wasn't? Zoey spent most of her toddler years sticky and covered in snot. But the amount of the money order was meager, sufficient for a few days of groceries. Maybe that was all she needed. Or maybe that was all she had.

Aaugh! Alma could feel herself getting agitated. She needed to stop. She wasn't there to solve other people's problems, especially when she couldn't deal with her own. Mona would be done soon enough, then she could help the woman, at which point Stan would come back and chew Alma out for whatever indiscretion he felt she committed.

Like letting him know you were quitting by not showing up to work and leaving another clerk to work your shift, without her diabetes medicine.

Alma grabbed her purse and pulled out her wallet. She found two twenty-dollar bills and handed them to the woman.

"Here you go. Have a nice day."

"But...," the woman stuttered, utterly confounded.

"We're having a cash-back special on all money orders," Alma said quickly.

The woman still hesitated though.

Alma blew a noisy breath out of her

mouth. "Just go, okay?"

The young mother was still confused when she walked away, but she accepted the cash.

Alma dove back into her purse and pulled out the cloth napkin she had tossed in there that morning. Unraveling it, she revealed a hummingbird necklace. The chain was long and tangled, but the bird itself was in pristine shape. It was made from metal and inset with costume jewelry. Truth be told, it was completely worthless, but Alma still loved it, as did Zoey. The little girl had begged her aunt for it, promising to care for it as her own. Alma wasn't so sure then, but she had no doubt her niece would do so now.

Wrapping it back up carefully, Alma placed it in the package, along with a note for Leta. Then she sealed the envelope, slapped some postage on it and dropped it in the outgoing mail. With another item on her list completed, Alma fixed her attention on Mona who was hanging up the phone. The older woman finished scribbling her notes before turning back around.

"So…my paycheck?" Alma reminded her.

Mona offered her a scornful look and shook her head. But she retrieved the paycheck from the top drawer.

"Can you cash it, please?" Alma asked, plastering the most innocent looking smile on her face. "Oh, and this too," she added, handing her the money order.

"What's that?" Mona looked it over. "What is this? Your name's not on it."

"I know. I had a little trouble doing your job. Can you just cash them so I can get out of here before Stan gets back?"

This time, Mona's frustration was real. She tightened her lips and turned around, check and money order in hand. Without a word, she processed both, counting the money out, once, twice, three times. Alma was impatient by this point. Stan was sure to walk in any moment and catch her there. The check was hers, he couldn't withhold it from her. But the last thing Alma wanted was a chastisement.

Mona finally finished counting out the money. Alma grabbed it and apologized.

"Sorry. Thanks for everything," she sputtered, snatched her purse and ran towards the door. She was shoving the cash into her bag when she crashed into someone else and came to a very sudden and unexpected stop. She would have fallen back if arms hadn't caught her and wrapped themselves around her, pulling her into an upright position. She was snuggled closely to a male chest, and as she glanced up at the face attached to the body, her first thought was, *Oh no.*

IT WAS a longshot, but Noah decided to go to the supermarket on Third Street. He didn't expect to find Alma, but he had to try. Yes, try; or else Cass would never let him be. She would hound him and when she was done, she would drag him to the store to inquire about the woman. She meant well, he was sure, but Cass was too much sometimes. Especially when it was his life she was meaning well about.

Noah pulled into a parking spot in the middle of the lot and exited his car. He locked it and slowly made his way to the store. With a deep breath, he prepared himself for failure.

And what he would tell Cass when he got back.

I tried, he practiced. What more did he need to say?

His phone buzzed in his pocket as he neared the entrance. Noah pulled it out and glanced at the screen.

Cass.

Well, speak of the devil, he thought, momentarily distracted. He didn't see anyone when he stepped through the doors. So, when his body connected with another—a woman—he was surprised, but quick to react. Instinctively, he put his arms around her and steadied her, so she wouldn't fall. Only then did he get a better look at the woman. It was Alma. Every doubt and thought of failure he had entertained was erased the moment he locked eyes with her.

Then she opened her mouth.

"Why are you here?" she demanded.

Noah wasn't sure, but Alma didn't sound too happy to see him. He had rather hoped she would be.

"How did you find me?" she asked as she pulled herself out of his embrace.

An older woman walked up behind them, reminding Noah they were blocking the doorway.

Seems I've been doing that all day.

He took hold of Alma's elbow and moved them out of the way.

"I wanted to see you," he said.

Alma frowned and crossed her arms over her chest. She eyed him carefully, as if looking for an ulterior motive. Noah didn't know what to make of her reaction, especially when she said, "You've seen me. Is that it?"

Flabbergasted, he exclaimed, "No, that's not it. What about this morning?"

"What about it?" Her tone was flat.

Noah was getting ready to tell her how amazing their kiss was, how it was all he thought about in his downtime since then, how he loved the way she fit in his arms and tasted on his lips…but they were interrupted.

"Alma?"

Both Noah and Alma turned their heads in the direction of the voice. At the end of the sidewalk in front of the store was a middle-aged man with a smoothie in his hand. He was waving at them and seemed about as happy to see Alma as she did to see Noah.

"Alma?" he called again.

In response, she grabbed Noah's arm and pulled him in front of her.

"Did you drive?" she asked him.

"What?"

"Did. You. Drive." She spoke through clenched teeth.

"Yes."

She pushed him towards the parking lot. Noah didn't understand what was happening, but he knew enough to recognize she wanted to get away from the man, who was now following them.

"Where's your car?" he asked, huffing along.

"Don't have one."

"What's going on?"

But Alma only pushed him along, faster and faster. They were close to breaking out into a run when they finally reached his car.

"Here, here," he said, pulling his keys out of his pocket. He unlocked the doors and dove in, Alma beside him. He tossed his phone into the console and started the car.

"Go, go, go," she said with urgency as the man ran up to them. Noah backed up, careful not to hit him, then drove off. It wasn't until they exited the parking lot that Alma breathed a little easier. Noah was still on edge though, as Glen's words of warning flashed through his mind.

Seven

ALMA COULD HEAR THE agitation in Noah's voice as he yelled, "What the hell was that about?"

"Nothing," she replied, nonchalantly.

"That was *not* nothing! Who was that?"

She shrugged her shoulders and moved her purse onto her lap.

"My boss. Trust me, it really was nothing."

Alma pulled out the money Mona gave her and began counting it. She was out ten dollars after balancing the money order against her paycheck, but no matter. There was still quite a bit left. More than enough actually.

Noah's quick breaths drew her out of her thoughts. She glanced at him and saw he was close to hyperventilating. He muttered, "Oh God, oh God, oh God," under his breath, while his eyes darted between her and the road.

"What's wrong with you?" Alma asked.

"You robbed the place, didn't you?"

Alma laughed. She had been accused of a lot of things in her life, but never robbery. She supposed the circumstances did lend themselves to that conclusion, but never would she have assumed it.

"Relax," she said, putting the money away. She placed her purse by her feet and turned towards him. "I didn't rob the place, okay? That was my pay."

"So why did you run?" Noah asked, his tone defensive.

"He wanted to have a few words with me regarding my decision to quit earlier this week, but I didn't want to talk to him."

Noah huffed and puffed, while his face turned red, and his forehead wrinkled up. He looked at her, eyed the road, then turned to her once more. Alma could see he wanted to argue, but she was pretty sure he might pass out too. She watched him intently, curious to see which one would occur first.

Instead, Noah changed lanes, pulled into a gas station and parked the car. He took several deep breaths, and then turned towards her. Alma was almost disappointed that he didn't pass out; of course, she didn't know what she would have done if he did, so maybe it was good.

"We got off on the wrong foot," he said, obviously willing himself calm. "Let's start again."

"Actually, I think we're fine...," Alma started, but stopped when she saw his face turning red again. It was cute, but she really didn't want to upset him.

"I'm Noah," he stated through pursed lips.

"I know. It's on your name tag," she replied, pointing to his shirt.

He bit his lower lip, then said, "And you're Alma."

She had been too amused to care about the fact that he was messing up her plans, but now that he had identified her, she needed to know how he had found her. "Yeah, so how do you know that?" she asked. "And how did you know where to find me? Are you stalking me?"

Noah glared at her with incredulity, then laughed.

"Weren't you the one who walked into the bookstore this morning and…you know, kissed me?"

Dammit, he was right.

"Okay, so turnaround is fair play, fine. How did you find me?"

"Your tattoo. We called around to all the shops in the area, ended up talking to a guy named Glen."

Alma arched an eyebrow.

"Glen told you where to find me?"

Noah nodded. "He said to tell you he was the one who told me."

"That son-of-a-bitch," Alma muttered.

The man, intimidating as he was, was always reserved. He knew her more intimately than most people did and though their relationship hadn't gone beyond drunken sex, she had always assumed he had her back. That he willingly told Noah then bragged about it only served to upset her.

"What else did he tell you?" she asked with disdain. Noah probably had all sorts of preconceived notions in his head now thanks to Glen.

"Only that you're trouble," he responded, though hesitantly.

Alma waited for more, but that was all he said.

"That's it?"

Noah nodded his head, then added, "Is he right?"

Alma chuckled. "What do you think?"

He opened his mouth but seemed to rethink whatever it was he was going to say. He stared at her with dark, chocolate eyes that seemed to take in every inch of her. Alma didn't feel violated as much as she felt intrigued. He was overwhelmed, the reaction she often got from those around her. She was a handful and Noah was just another victim of her sometimes manic personality. So how would he respond?

"I don't know," he finally said.

Alma's heart melted just a little bit with that admission. Perhaps…

No, he doesn't fit into your life, she reminded herself. Alma conceded and sat back, as if the distance would harden her heart again.

"So," she said, changing the focus. "All this trouble just to get my name, huh?"

"Well, you did come out of the blue this morning." He reached into his pocket and pulled out a piece of paper. "You left this too, I think."

Her eyes widened when she saw it was her list and she quickly grabbed it.

"What's all that?" he asked.

"Nothing," she said, curtly as she folded the paper up and placed it in her purse. She squared her shoulders and held her head up, closing herself off once more. He seemed dazed once again, more so than before, but said nothing. Silence filled the car again, accompanied by awkwardness. Alma stared at the gas pump across the lot, looking for a distraction.

"I want to see you," he finally said.

She shook her head, and said, "I don't think so." She didn't even bother looking at him, knowing she might change her mind if she did.

"Why not? Are you seeing someone? Glen?"

"No." Her answer came out with more indignation than she intended, "Why can't I just *not* want to see you?"

"Because you kissed me?"

She grinned, remembering the kiss—warm, wet, sweet...

"Why did you kiss me?" he asked. Alma could hear the hesitation in his voice. She turned to him, his eyes begging her for an explanation. She would have thought it obvious, but one look at his face told her it wasn't. He couldn't see how adorably appealing he was. He really was cute; there was something about his innocent and thoughtful nature that made him indescribably sexy. Maybe she should have asked first, but she couldn't chance him turning her away, not today. So, she stole what wasn't hers, a kiss.

Maybe she was a thief after all.

Of course, she wasn't going to tell him any of this; it would only go to his head. In her experience, that's how it worked with guys.

"Alma?"

"I don't know. Something to do," she said quickly. "Can we not do this?" she added, feeling trapped.

"You're the one who started it."

"I kissed you, that's all."

"Yeah, well, that's not exactly something normal people go around doing."

"So, I'm not normal?"

"I didn't mean that."

"That's what it sounded like."

"Look, can we just stop?" He was flustered again. "Let's forget about the kiss. I mean, not forget. I just thought maybe there was something between us."

He looked at her pleadingly, but Alma offered nothing. She couldn't. This wasn't supposed to happen. Just a kiss and that's it. Nothing more. So what if he was right. There could be nothing else.

"Well, wasn't there?" he continued.

She shrugged her shoulders and stared at her fingernails.

"Alma?"

She studied them more intently.

"Will you go to dinner with me at least? We don't have to do anything more if you don't want to," he begged.

Dropping the feigned interest in her manicure, she sat up and leaned into the console, towards him. "I'm bad news," she whispered. "You'll regret the day you met me."

Noah shook his head.

"Never."

Alma stared into his eyes. She didn't

want to give in, because she knew how the day would end. And Noah seemed too nice of a guy for her. But she could see he wasn't going to stop. And since he had gone to so much trouble to mess up her plans, then she should say yes and let him take out to dinner—and everywhere else she needed to go. Maybe she would have a little fun with him too.

"Just dinner, nothing more," Alma finally said, "But we need to make a few stops first."

Eight

"I REALLY NEED TO GET BACK to work," Noah stated, as they got out of his car. They were at a strip mall in the opposite side of town. There was no strewn garbage or graffiti, like the other neighborhood. It was clean and upper class. But despite the positive changes, Noah was still out of his element.

"You've been out most of the day; what's the rush now?" Alma asked.

She had a point.

"Well, I thought Glen would kill me, so it almost didn't matter. Now that I'm still alive though, I'd like to remain employed."

Alma chuckled and slung her purse over her head.

"He's a teddy bear," she said as she pushed her hair back. Then, without waiting on him, she skipped towards the door of the boutique she wanted to visit. Noah didn't agree with her assessment of Glen, but he didn't argue. "Just call them," she advised.

"And tell them what?"

Noah remained at a loss—for words and thoughts— when it came to Alma. Yes, he wanted to see her and was thrilled she had agreed to dinner with him, but at the cost of his job? Cass and Jada could only cover for so long. How was he supposed to explain this to Bill?

Alma didn't answer him though. She held the door open for him and smiled. "Are you coming?" she asked. She held her hand out to him, and smiled, a broad, infectious smile. She was beautiful. Breathtakingly so. And Noah couldn't say no to her. He locked his car and ran up to her.

The shop was a high-end boutique, specializing in women's clothes and accessories. The ambiance was light, springy; while the store itself was spacious and inviting. Noah wanted to run. He was sorely out of place. He didn't know the first thing about women's fashion. He didn't know anything about fashion, period. Most of his wardrobe consisted of t-shirts he had acquired at the bookstore.

"Can I help you?"

A middle-aged woman with red hair and matching lipstick greeted them from behind the counter. She had a smile on her face, but her eyes moved carefully between them. Noah could only imagine what she was thinking.

"Why yes," Alma piped up. "I would like to purchase a dress. It's a special day for me." She grabbed Noah's hand and pulled him further into the store. He was once again overwhelmed as she dragged him around, choosing the dress she was interested in. The clerk had lost some of her hesitation and asked, "Would you like to try this on?"

"Please," Alma replied, still hanging onto him.

They were led to a fitting room in the back, no larger than a closet, with three side-by-side mirrors and a plush armchair in the corner. Alma let go of Noah's hand and walked straight in, leaving him standing in the hallway, feeling awkward. He had never gone shopping with Sage, or shared this type of experience with anyone, so he was unsure of what to do. There was no chair or bench outside the room and everything around him was feminine and intimidating. He cursed himself for a moment, wondering why he was so inept around women, when his phone buzzed. Grateful for the reprieve, he didn't even care that it was Cass again.

"'Where are you?'" she asked, her voice low.

"It's a long story," he replied in an equally low tone.

"'Well, did you find her?'"

"Yeah...," he began and instinctively turned towards Alma.

"'So, what's her name?'"

Noah's mouth opened, but no words came out, not even sounds, for Alma had kicked off her shoes and was unbuttoning her shorts. He should have walked away then and there, for decency's sake, but he couldn't. He knew what was coming next and no matter how hard he tried, he couldn't pull away from the sight in front of him.

"'Noah…'"

Not even Cass' voice was enough to distract him. He simply kept watching Alma, her lovely image reflected in the mirror. Her shorts dropped to the floor, showing off a pair of lacy white panties that covered her beautifully rounded and well-packed posterior.

Then she reached down and pulled the bottom of her shirt up and over her head, revealing her bare breasts.

Oh my God, were the only words Noah could piece together. *She's not wearing a bra, she's not wearing a bra.*

The room suddenly felt hotter, as his shorts became more constricted. He knew he should close his eyes, turn away, move, out of civility's sake, because he was a decent guy (he was!), but he was glued to his spot on the floor, there outside the change room, where he could see her large, round breasts and her taut, peaked nipples. Noah had to adjust himself as he caught full view of Alma's tattoo—hummingbirds feeding on a vine that began behind her ear, descended her neck, entwined itself around her shoulder and upper arm and cradled her breast. It was stunning.

As if oblivious of his presence, Alma moved to the chair and picked up the dress. It was a cream-colored floral-print gown, a perfect complement to her tanned skin. Because it was strapless, Alma carefully stepped into it and pulled it up to her waist, then over her breasts, adjusting the elastic so that it fit her perfectly. Noah was mesmerized. Not that he had never seen a naked woman before…a gloriously nude woman who was perfect in shape and form…

"Wow," was the only thing he could manage, though it came out more like a grunt.

God, he was a caveman now.

"'Noah!'"

He broke from his thoughts as Cass yelled in his ear. Afraid Alma would hear her, he quickly turned away. He could feel his face turning red and his erection…well, it was pretty obvious, considering he had spent what felt like an eternity watching Alma.

"'Hello!'"

Noah adjusted himself again and

wandered back through the store. He needed to focus on anything but Alma, but it proved to be a fruitless effort: everything reminded him of her, from the floral prints similar to the ones she wore, to the leafy jewelry that would complement her choice of clothing.

"'Noah, what's her name?'"

Before he could say anything at all, he caught sight of Alma once again, now chatting with the sales clerk at the front counter, still wearing the dress, accompanied now by a modest set of heels and leafy earrings, not unlike the ones he had touched just minutes earlier. She turned her head towards him and smiled, causing him to ache once again.

Noah was in trouble.

LETA WAITED patiently in the carpool line as it crept forward. This was her daily ritual. As a stay-at-home mom, her primary responsibility was her daughter Zoey and her husband Owen. She got up early to fix breakfast and pack lunches. She made sure the household was maintained and everything was perfect for her perfect family; and this included being at the school when the end-of-day bell rang. Sure, Zoey was old enough to ride the bus, but she didn't feel comfortable allowing her soon-to-be eight-year-old to do so yet. Her husband Owen argued that she was coddling their only child, but Leta knew better.

The car in front of Leta drove forward a few feet, then stopped. Leta did the same. She considered all she still had to do (*just call me Superwoman*, she thought), recalling the items she had listed in her datebook this morning. Among them was Zoey's upcoming birthday party. They were going to host a salon party: Zoey and several of her friends were going to get manicures and pedicures to celebrate her eighth birthday.

A few cars drove off, clearing the way for Leta to pull up to the front of the line. After giving her daughter's name to the teacher with the walkie-talkie, Leta sat back and waited for Zoey. Minutes later, the little girl hurried excitedly to the car, carrying her backpack and lunch bag. She was smiling and talking rapidly as she got in and buckled up.

"Whoa, slow down Zoey," Leta said, pulling forward and out of the carpool line. "I take it you had a good day."

"It was the best," she exclaimed. "All my friends said they're coming to the party."

Leta smiled proudly.

"I'm glad to hear that."

"It's going to be so much fun."

"Yes, it will be. And guess what? Your Nana is coming."

"She is?"

"And she's bringing your cousins with her," Leta stated, driving away from the school. She rattled off the names of Owen's nieces, paying attention to the road as she spoke. "You are going to have lots of fun."

"Can *Tia* Alma come?"

Leta came to a stop at a light. Then she exhaled heavily. Zoey was unaware of Alma's troubled past; as well she should be since she was so young. But it made the situation difficult, considering Alma was still family. Truthfully, there were times Leta wanted to deny she had a sister, but she never did. Instead she did what most good Latinas were known for and handled everything with tact and finesse.

Forget Superwoman; I could run a small country with these skills.

"*Mami?*"

"I don't think that would be a good idea, *querida*."

"Why not?"

"Because Alma is…" Leta thought about the excuses she always gave, the cover-up she offered for her sister's actions. She considered all the trouble Alma had brought them in the past year alone. She had sheltered Zoey from much of it, but still the little girl adored her wayward aunt. And Leta doubted Zoey would take her word if she told her the absolute truth about Alma. This didn't leave much in the way of explanation that her precious daughter would accept. "It's just not a good idea, Zoey. Let's leave it at that."

"But why can't she come see us? You're the one who always tells me to try to get along with everyone. Why don't you get along with her?"

Leta eyed her daughter in the rearview mirror, as she pulled into traffic and headed home. The child listened, that was good; but she was too smart for her own good.

"It's a long story baby. Let's talk about something else, okay?"

Zoey sighed and slumped back in her seat, obviously disappointed with her response.

"Why don't you tell me about your class?" Leta said, in an effort to distract her.

Her daughter responded dutifully, telling her about her work, her friends and her teacher. Leta kept her talking until they got home.

"Alright, you know the drill. Go get changed then come downstairs to do homework, okay?"

Zoey nodded and did as she was told. Leta watched her go, knowing she would eventually have to tell her the truth about Alma.

Nine

WAR AND PEACE.
To Kill a Mockingbird.
The Great Gatsby.
Animal Farm.

Noah tried to fill his mind with as many literary titles as he could think of to distract him from Alma, who had settled in comfortably in the passenger seat beside him as they continued onto their next destination.

Lord of the Flies.

Gone with the Wind.

Romeo and Juliet.

No, not Romeo and Juliet. It's a romance…sort of. Think of the Bible, yes, the Bible.

Since leaving the boutique, they stopped at the bank to make a withdrawal (Alma gleefully assured him she didn't rob it) and then stopped for a quick snack at the gas station where she loaded up on nachos and a smoothie. She certainly had a healthy appetite and a cheerful disposition, if not a blind one, ignoring the many men who were gawking at her. Noah wondered if he should perhaps show some sign of disapproval for all the whistles and catcalls, but part of him wondered if she wasn't enjoying the attention.

Frankenstein.

The Catcher in The Rye.

Wuthering Heights.

Grapes of Wrath.

"Right up here," she directed.

Noah focused on the road. He followed the flow of traffic to a one-way street, then turned into a parking lot at Alma's instruction. He wasn't sure where they were going, but it didn't matter at this point. He had skipped out on work and voluntarily become Alma's lackey, thinking only of her body instead of how he was going to explain his hours-long lunch break to Bill. As it was, he found himself too concerned with his lack of morals. He had done and said more that was out of character for him since meeting Alma; and the worst part of it all, he almost didn't care.

"Here we are," she chirped unbuckling her seat belt before he even came to a stop. Noah found a vacant spot and parked there. He looked around the area for some indication of where he was, but there was nothing, except for an old sign warning others not to trespass.

"Where are we?" he asked, but Alma had already exited the car. Noah sighed and followed her along a rocky path to the fence surrounding the lot. His phone vibrated in his pocket. Certain it was Cass calling for more details, he ignored it. He and Alma slipped through a large hole in the fence and stepped onto a sidewalk. Noah had never been to this side of town before and could only imagine what he was walking into. Certainly, it was better than the neighborhood Glen's shop was located in but given the condition of the lot and the fence, Noah knew it wasn't by much. He caught up to Alma as they came to a stop at the corner. She smiled at him and took his hand. Together, they crossed the street when the light turned red.

It was strangely weird, but nice.

"Where are we going?" Noah asked. He didn't expect a response, having received none before. But she surprised him this time when she said, "The homeless shelter."

This was the last response he expected. Now he really did feel guilty for gawking at her earlier.

The shelter was located in an older building that had once been a church. There was a tall spire and a steeple atop the roof. The shadow of a cross long removed adorned the façade of the building, covered instead by the name of the shelter. The grounds were in similar condition as the parking lot: the hedges needed trimming and litter hid in the crevices of the stairs. Noah slowed his strides for a moment as they began bounding the steps, but Alma only pulled him along.

They entered the front door and walked past the receptionist, who lifted her head briefly. Apparently satisfied it was Alma, she resumed staring at the computer screen in front of her. They continued past several offices and a door labeled 'stairs'. Before Noah could inquire about anything, Alma pulled him through the door and down the stairs.

"Hey Alma," a voice greeted them as they exited the stairwell.

"Hi Wade," Alma replied, letting go of Noah's hand to hug the man in front of her. He was middle-aged with a receding hairline and round belly, no different than Bill, but a lot happier, Noah thought.

"Who's your friend?"

"This is Noah," she said proudly. "We're going to dinner."

Wade lifted an eyebrow and parted his lips, as if he wanted to say something, but he did not and extended his hand instead.

"Nice to meet you."

Noah shook his hand, firmly, quickly, not sure if he was indeed happy to meet another of Alma's acquaintances. This was turning into a day of show-and-tell; and he was the object of attention.

Wade turned back to Alma.

"So, you're giving him our deluxe tour?" he asked.

"Actually, I'm looking for Saad," she replied. "Is he around?"

Wade rubbed the back of his head and thought for a moment.

"I haven't seen him today."

Alma frowned, disappointed.

"Of course, I've been running errands. And it is almost dinner time, so I'm sure he's somewhere around here," Wade offered.

"Can I check?" she asked.

He looked at Noah skeptically, which only added to the confusion of the moment. Noah wondered what exactly was going through his head. Finally, Wade took in a deep breath and turned to Alma.

"Yeah, no problem. Just be quick, okay?"

Her frown disappeared and she threw her arms around the older man in appreciation.

"Thanks Wade," she squealed, then just as quickly released him, grabbed Noah's hand once again and skipped down the hall. He ran with her past the kitchen and the dining room before she stopped to get her bearings.

"What are we doing here?" he asked. Again. It seemed this was all he had been doing that afternoon.

"Trying to find Saad," she said, looking around.

"Who's Saad?"

"A friend."

She continued walking again.

"And… it's important to find him now?" Noah asked.

Alma didn't reply; instead she glanced into the recreational room, outfitted with a pool table and a small television in the corner, where several men in their late sixties, Noah guessed, were seated. She smiled and released his hand so she could walk over to them. He didn't follow, partly because he wanted to give her space to do what she came to do, but also because the situation was uncomfortable enough.

"Well hello there, beautiful," one man said, with a toothless grin.

Alma stopped and posed for him, a hand on her hip, a bountiful leg peeking out of the cut in her skirt.

Noah turned around and took a deep breath.

"Hanging out with us lowlifes today?" he heard the same man ask. Noah turned back around. Alma was resting on the arm of the chair, while the man had his arm around her waist. The other two had leaned in, presumably to get a better look at her. Noah felt his face warm; he didn't like this.

"Come on, boys. That would make me a lowlife too," she sassed.

"Not you, baby," another one said.

The third man agreed.

"Oh, you guys...," she gushed, sickeningly saccharine.

"What are you doing here?" the first one asked.

"To see you, of course. You know I couldn't stay away." She stood up and put her arm around one of the other men. Each of them rose to their feet and swarmed her, making complimentary and lewd remarks at her...at least what Noah considered lewd between several older men and a young beautiful woman, who didn't notice or didn't care that she was being hit on. There seemed to be some kind of chemistry between them that Alma was unsettlingly comfortable with. She treated them no different than someone who was not in their situations and appeared to lap up the attention they were giving her— every crude and sexual bit of it. Of course, Noah didn't know these men and he didn't know exactly what was going on, so he couldn't judge. But it sure didn't seem right.

"Listen, guys, since I'm here," Alma began, as she reached into her purse and pulled out the currency envelope she received from the bank. "This is for you."

No one was flirting now: the men grew quiet as she counted out several large bills and handed them to the man in the chair she had been sharing. She did the same two more times, conferring the money to the other two men as she did with the first. They looked as confounded as Noah felt.

"What's this?"

"A gift," Alma said simply.

"Nah, doll. I can't take this," the third man said handing it back to her. She withdrew her hands though and insisted, "Look, I don't need it, okay? Just take it."

He held his hand out for a moment before pulling it back. Silence filled the air as each man looked to one another, then back to Alma. Noah thought they might refuse her once more, but he didn't get to find out—his phone started buzzing again. He quickly pulled it out of his pocket and turned back into the hallway.

"Hello?" he whispered.

"Where the hell are you?" the voice on the other end growled.

Noah cringed: it was Bill.

"Bill, I—"

"I don't pay you to go chasing skirts."

"I'm not, listen—"

"I pay you to stock shelves and sell books."

"I understand, but—"

"Get your ass back here, or you're fired!"

Noah didn't even try to argue, namely because Bill had hung up; but he was expecting this. More than that, Noah deserved to get chewed out. He had gone AWOL. God only knew if he still had a job. Bill's tone was dreadful, but his words were hopeful that if Noah left now, he might have something to return to. Maybe if he explained about Alma and how he couldn't say no to her and how he was her ride. Plus, he actually found the courage to ask her to dinner and she said yes. How could he just leave her after all that?

Noah sighed. He should just plan to start looking for another job as soon as the date concluded. At least he had enough money to pay for dinner.

Wait, do I?

He did some quick math in his head and even though they hadn't chosen a location to dine at, he figured he should have enough money for tonight. Of course, if things went well, there might be a second and third date, in which case he would have to get employed soon. Then again, Alma didn't seem to be hurting for cash, maybe… No, he was a gentleman. He would pay for everything. He was the one who asked Alma out.

Speaking of which...

Noah pocketed his phone and turned around to see if Alma was finished flirting with and giving money to the three raunchy, homeless men.

That sounds so bad, he thought; and nearly missed Alma as she grabbed his arm and pulled him into the hallway.

"Come on," she said, hurriedly.

Noah looked over his shoulder to see if anyone was pursuing them again. No one was.

"What?"

"Come on," was all she said though.

"What about the guys...what about them?" he asked, struggling to keep up with her.

"What about them?"

She entered one of the classrooms and shut the door behind them. He looked around at the empty chairs and desks, wondering what they were doing here. He turned back to Alma, searching for an answer, but her whole disposition had changed: she looked like a hungry tiger about to pounce on its prey. Unprepared for this, Noah took a couple of steps back. Feeling silly and slightly emasculated, he stepped back up as she approached him. She was face-to-face, toe-to-toe with him, her hands on his chest, breathing heavy. Or maybe he was. He couldn't tell. Her lips so close to his, he could taste her breath. There wasn't much Noah could do to stop from going hard with desire.

"What are you doing?" he asked. It was the same question he had been asking all afternoon.

Alma slid her hand down his chest to his erect manhood.

"This," she said, and before he could pull away from her, she kissed him. Mouth open, her tongue seeking his, Alma brazenly smothered his senses. Hands roaming, fingers touching, Noah was helpless against her and quickly gave up the fight. She felt exquisite. She smelled exquisite. She tasted...

Still kissing, Alma pushed him back, one awkward step after another, until he hit the blackboard with a thud, causing a small cloud of chalk to rise. Alma pulled away. Temporarily distracted, Noah didn't see her drop to her knees in front of him. Only when she had unzipped his shorts and had begun pulling them down did he realize what she was doing. Shocked, Noah moved away from Alma.

She rose to her feet and with a smug smile on her face, moved closer to him. He took another step away from her but bumped into a podium. He was trapped with his shorts around his ankles and nowhere to go.

"You're so cute when you're shy," she cooed.

"What?"

"Come on, Noah. Isn't this what you wanted? This whole time following me around, undressing me with your eyes, watching me back at the boutique…"

Noah's face grew hot with embarrassment.

"Uh, no, yes. No," he stammered. "I haven't been undressing you. No."

"Oh, I think that's a yes," she said as she ran her finger down his jawline. "It's okay, though. I want you too," she added with a whisper. She moved in to kiss him again and even though the promise of sex, one way or another, was very tempting, Noah couldn't do this. He had never gone past first base on a first date, if that's what he and Alma were doing. Even with Sage, it wasn't until their third date he dared moving onto second base. Of course, the fact that he still referred to the natural progression of an intimate relationship as 'bases' was probably the reason he was still a virgin and woefully out of his depths when it came to someone like Alma, who obviously mistook his gawking as a signal that he wanted sex. He was a guy, so yeah, he did, but not now and not like this.

Noah grabbed his shorts off the floor and held them to his waist. Then he squared his shoulders and stuck out his chin.

"No," he ordered confidently, though he didn't feel it.

She looked up at him, eyebrow arched, hand on her hip, attitude abounding.

"No?"

Noah cringed; she sounded offended.

"Look, I'm not going to deny that I find you attractive …very attractive..." His voice squeaked. Why did his voice squeak? How was he supposed to exude confidence with a squeaky voice? "But we can't do this. I mean, I would like to, don't get me wrong, but I'm not trying to jump into bed. You're more than that. I want to have dinner with you. I want to get to know you."

"I told you, there's nothing after dinner."

Noah frowned: she had mentioned this earlier, but he naively thought she meant the physical aspect of a date. Did she really want nothing from him? Yes, this was the most atypical first date he had been on, but could it be she had already decided there was nothing else? Why continue then? Why go to dinner? Why pretend? Why did she go after him then?

"So…what is this then?"

He couldn't hide his disappointment.

Much good it did him though: she simply crossed her arms over her chest and looked away.

"Alma…?"

She flared her nostrils and took in a deep breath. For a moment, Noah thought she might end it right there, walk away, leave him standing in the classroom of the shelter holding his pants up, wondering if he had done right by rejecting her advances. But she didn't. She finally turned back to him. There was a momentary flash of vulnerability in her eyes that was quickly replaced with cynicism, as she stoically stated, "I'm hungry. Let's go."

Ten

ALMA PEERED INTO THE DIMLY-lit bathroom mirror. Her eye make-up was smudged, and her long hair was bothering her. Frustrated, she pulled out her make-up case and hairbrush. She cleaned up the smudges and applied a thick coating of black eye-liner. Then she brushed her hair back into a messy-bun. She stared at herself again, her eyes bold and commanding. She liked the look, liked the way it made her feel.

Just like sex. Alma had always been comfortable in her skin, enjoying the way her body was soft, round and feminine. She was made for sex; she appreciated and loved it. Sometimes it even drove her, but nothing so consuming that she trolled clubs and street corners looking for a quick lay. She just loved the adrenaline rush she got from it. So, for Noah to deny her…

You scared him, she chastised herself. *You came on too strong. You always come on too strong.*

The argument in her head quickly became fuddled.

No, I don't.

Sure you do. Remember Finn?

No. We're not discussing Finn.

If he can't accept this is me…

He doesn't want you now because he thinks you're too easy. Finn, Noah, Finn, Noah… they all do.

No they don't.

You are easy.

No, I'm not.

Besides, it's not like it matters.

You are crazy!

Yeah, that helps…name-calling.

"Aaugh!" she yelled, then looked around. No one was in there with her. Yet, she felt stupid for letting her emotions get the best of her. This is not the way her day was supposed to end. Besides, she still had dinner with Noah to get through.

He had been silent all the way from the homeless shelter to the restaurant. He was a naturally quiet person, but this…this was something different. He didn't look at her once with those rich, chocolatey eyes, nor did he give her any of the attention he had willfully offered earlier. He was upset.

It wasn't my fault. I told him, dinner and that's it.

It is your fault. You should have just let him be.

Rather than give into another battle of words, Alma collected her things, shoved them back into her purse and exited the restroom. Once she was in the hallway, she took a deep breath and collected herself. She made her way from the hall to the dining room, where Noah was waiting for her. They had been seated earlier by the hostess; and almost immediately, Alma excused herself to the restroom. With no other place to go to, she returned to the table. Noah was perusing the menu when she sat down. He glanced at her briefly then resumed what he was doing.

Alma took that as her cue and began browsing through the menu, though she was familiar with the cuisine.

"Their crab cakes here are awesome…for a bar," Alma advised.

Noah nodded, but said nothing.

Their waiter appeared. Dressed in all black, he set a plate of bread on the table and greeted them.

"Would you like to hear our specials for tonight?"

"Sure."

He ran down the list of food, but Alma didn't listen. She knew what she was going to order. Instead she looked around. The room was dim and there was a band playing in the corner, no different than the last time she had been there…with Finn. This was their regular spot for dinner, drinks and fun…then. Now, she wasn't supposed to be here, but she had one more item to cross off her list.

"Do you want me to come back?" the waiter inquired.

Alma shook her head, pulling out of her thoughts. She looked up at him and offered him a flirty smile.

"I'll have the crab cakes with a glass of red wine. Will that work?"

"Yes, ma'am. And you, sir?"

Both Alma and the waiter turned to Noah. He seemed to be caught unaware and looked up at the waiter in surprise.

"Uh, I'll have the same. Get me a beer though."

"Absolutely," the waiter replied, picked up the menus and walked away.

Alma commented, "I was going to say, you don't look like a red wine type of guy."

"It's not my thing."

"Well, to each his own, right?"

He shrugged his shoulders, still upset.

You were clear—nothing past dinner. If he wants to be upset, that's his deal, Alma told herself. She wasn't going to give in to his tantrum. Instead, she picked up the small loaf of bread in front of her and cut into it.

"So how long have you worked in that bookstore?" she asked making small talk. "You don't look like a reader to me."

"I'm not," he replied. "Last time I picked

up a book to read was probably in high school."

She slathered the bread with butter and bit into it.

"So why work in a bookstore?" she continued.

"It's a job," he muttered as he picked up the other half of the loaf and transferred it to his plate.

"Fair enough," Alma agreed and kept on eating.

"So, what was this morning about?" he asked.

"What do you mean?"

"The kiss?"

"Oh, that," Alma mumbled. She didn't want to discuss the kiss anymore. She didn't regret it, for he was a good kisser and well, she rather enjoyed it, but it was unfortunate he kept pushing for more.

The waiter returned with their drinks. She offered him an attentive smile and a bat of her eyelashes. He asked if there was anything else he could bring them.

"We're good, thanks," she replied, with a wink of her eye and watched him retreat to the kitchen.

"Okay, so what was that about?" Noah asked with obvious disdain in his voice.

"What?"

Alma could feel her pulse racing now,

like she did something wrong.

"Right there? You were flirting with him."

"That? I was just having fun," she responded dismissively.

"Just like this morning…"

"Maybe. Why are you getting all huffy about it?"

"Oh, I don't know. I thought there was a connection between us, but all you've been doing is flirting with the waiter and the homeless guys and don't even get me started on Glen. What the hell? Why'd you even agree to dinner if you were gonna flirt with every guy we came across?"

Alma could feel her face flush.

"I told you, it was nothing, okay? Don't read into this."

Her response came out more defensive than she intended.

"Read into what?"

His tone was as defensive as hers. This 'date' was not going well.

"Just because I said yes to dinner doesn't mean there's something between us," she exclaimed. Noah started to object, but she cut him off. "Because this? This is just dinner. This is me being hungry and taking advantage of a guy who wants to go out with me. I never promised you anything more than that. In fact, I've had a busy enough day without you in it."

"I'm the one who drove you everywhere!" he retorted. "If it wasn't for me, you'd still be at the boutique, dress shopping."

"Screw you!"

"Yeah, you did that already too. Or at least you tried."

Alma's mouth fell open, but she couldn't think of anything else to say. Apparently neither could Noah because he blew out a noisy breath, and turned his gaze away from her, exasperated. He was right, but this wasn't something she was ready to admit. After all, he didn't know her. He was just some boy she stumbled upon, some guy she kissed, someone who didn't mean anything to her, not a damn thing. She didn't have to explain herself to him. If she didn't have a reason for being there at the restaurant, she'd have left in a heartbeat.

Silence reigned between them for a few awkward minutes. Their waiter returned to assure them their dinner would be out shortly, but neither spoke, only nodded their heads. The band continued playing, while patrons continued talking, eating and celebrating— doing whatever it was they came to do. Alma wanted to take back the evening, to settle the emotions running high between her and

Noah, but it seemed too late for that. She turned away from the table towards the kitchen. Suddenly her task didn't seem so important that she had to stay and suffer the indignity of doubt and hurt on this of all nights. Tears stung her eyes, but Alma didn't allow them to drop. She blinked them away quickly. Then she squared her shoulders and held her head up. Screw Noah and Finn and everyone else. She was leaving.

"So…why did you wear the dress out?" Noah suddenly asked.

The question took Alma by surprise.

"What?" she asked, turning to him.

"Why did you wear the dress out of the store?" he asked again. His tone, though, had changed: resignation, yes, but also curiosity. Alma met his eyes and saw something in them she didn't recognize.

"Oh, uh…" Every emotion she had entertained just seconds earlier seemed to drain out of her. "Laundry day?"

Noah smiled, small but sincere.

She elaborated, "I don't know. I really liked it and I wanted to wear it today."

Noah nodded. "It looks good on you," he said quietly.

Alma didn't understand how he could compliment her after being upset, but she didn't get a chance to think about it either: a waitress approached their table quickly, a frown marring her lovely face. Before Alma could inquire about her intentions, the woman picked up a glass of ice water and threw it in Alma's face. The shock caused her to gasp and choke on her breath. She jumped up, knocking her chair back.

"Bitch!" the waitress hissed, her face red with fury. "You know you're not supposed to be here."

Another waiter grabbed her by the waist and pulled her back. She fought him though, trying to get at Alma.

"Isn't it enough what you did to him? Get some self-respect and move on. He doesn't want you. Nobody does," she spewed.

The atmosphere in the place changed and everyone stopped to watch them. Even the band stopped playing. Wet and shocked, Alma looked around her, hot with embarrassment. Another waiter ran over to them, yelling, "Get Finn! Get Finn!"

"I'm going to call the police and they're gonna lock you up, just like you deserve," the woman continued, as she pulled her arm away from the man holding her back. Noah jumped in then, rushing to Alma's side to protect her from the waitress. "Crazy bitch!" she continued, before another voice interrupted them.

"Dawn!"

It was Finn. Both women turned towards him, but it was the waitress, Dawn, who had his attention. He wrapped his arms around her and pulled her away from the table, not once making eye contact with Alma. Her heart sank to the pit of her stomach.

"Stop, alright? Just stop," he encouraged Dawn.

"She isn't supposed to be here, Finn. That's what the court order said."

"It's alright," he said calmly. Alma watched as he handled the girl patiently, not once acknowledging her presence. She suddenly felt small and insignificant.

"It isn't right, what she did to you," Dawn argued.

"I know," he said, walking her away from the table. "But she's not worth it, Dawn. She's not worth it."

His last words, directed as Alma, hit their mark. Her eyes watered as she called out to him.

"Finn, wait!"

But he didn't. He kept on walking, leading Dawn away from *her* as if she was the one responsible for the outburst. Alma blinked, but she couldn't banish the tears away. One-by-one they streamed down her face as she realized all eyes were still on her, including Noah's.

"Alma?" he said, gently.

But everything had spiraled out of her control—Noah, her day, this dinner. And her one shot at redemption was gone. She was a complete and utter failure. This was it, she couldn't do it anymore, and without a word to Noah, who was still by her side, a confounded expression on his face, Alma grabbed her purse and rushed out of the restaurant.

Eleven

HE DOESN'T WANT YOU. NOBODY does. They're gonna lock you up, just like you deserve. She's not worth it. She's not worth it. Isn't it enough what you did to him? Get some self-respect and move on. He doesn't want you. Nobody does. She's not worth it. You're not worth it.

The words echoed in Alma's mind as she ran along the trail, down by the river's edge. Located a few blocks from the restaurant, the trail followed the contours of the river, the path illuminated by street lights above. There were people about her, couples, teenagers, vendors and such, but she ignored them as she ran, her breath heavy in her chest, tears running down her face. How could she think that seeing Finn would have gone any differently than it had? Granted, she hadn't expected the girlfriend—perhaps if she wasn't there, Finn would have been willing to speak to her. But as it was, Alma wasn't 'worth it.'

She's not worth it. She's not worth it, Finn had said, and after everything that happened between them, his viewpoint was understandable. She just wished she had the chance to make him see otherwise.

He's right, you know.

Shut up.

Alma slowed down her pace to a walk and worked to steady her breathing. Though she was considerably calmer than when she left the restaurant, she couldn't stop the tears from streaming down her face, leaving a salty trail behind. Nothing had gone right all day. In fact, it all went wrong the moment she kissed Noah.

It was wrong way before then. Just call it a night.

The tears ceased then. The voice was right—she had issues long before Noah. He was just a nice distraction. A pleasant one. He was everything she imagined him to be—cute and sweet and gentle and…safe. Not in the non-risk-taking way, but in the comfortable, bear-hug kind-of-way. She liked being around him. She liked the way he made her feel.

All the more reason to end it now. Things would have just gone badly, like they did with Finn. He doesn't want you after all. Nobody does.

Stop.

They're gonna lock you up, just like you deserve.

Stop!

End it now.

Stop! Stop! Stop!

Alma grabbed her head as if she could pull out the thoughts that were invading her peace. She closed her eyes and focused on the darkness. Still the words swirled around in her mind, damning her very existence. Swirling, spinning, until it was all she heard.

Her knees gave out from under her and Alma dropped to the ground, still holding her head, wanting only for the accusations to end.

Stop! Just stop! she commanded, but none heeded.

"Are you okay, Miss?"

The voice was so low Alma almost missed it. Only when she felt a hand on her shoulder did she realize someone else was there with her. She jerked back and looked up. A young woman, maybe college-age, dressed in a tank top and shorts was standing over her.

"Are you okay?" she repeated.

Alma dropped her arms and gazed past her, where a couple continued by them, though not without a glance backward.

"Yeah, I'm fine," Alma lied and thought to get up and leave before the scene escalated. Try as she might though, she couldn't get up. Her will to do so was gone. Instead she dropped down on her bottom and rested on the trail. Besides, where was she going to go? What was she going to do?

The woman crouched down and sat

beside her.

"Are you sure? Do you need a doctor or…someone?"

"I need a new life," Alma muttered mostly under her breath, but then she turned a cynical eye to the jogger. "If you have one of those, I'll gladly take it."

The woman chuckled, then asked, "Can I call someone for you?"

Alma shook her head.

"I've got nobody."

"Can I help you then?"

The woman gazed at her, the expression on her countenance soft. There was no pity that Alma could detect, yet there was something unnerving about the way she looked at her, filling Alma with an inexplicable sense of urgency.

"No one can help me," Alma stated, then stood up. "I gotta go."

The woman also rose to her feet.

"Are you going to be okay?" she asked.

Alma didn't respond, simply stepped away from her, towards the edge of the trail. She turned back once more to the woman, whose face was lit up with hope, something Alma no longer possessed. Part of her wanted to lash out at her, in spite and envy. But the other part knew that it was too late to hope: nothing would change.

Resuming her pace from before, Alma ran away from the woman, from the restaurant, from everything. The tears had dried up as had the errant emotions. Only one remained: anger—at the day for not going how she intended, at Finn for throwing her away again, at Noah for being there, at the woman, at everything and everyone. She was angry with God for giving her the short end of the stick when it came to who she was, angry at Leta for being different and not having to suffer as she did, angry, period. Alma knew better than anyone else that life wasn't fair, but did it have to be so devastatingly overwhelming?

Alma slowed her steps as she approached a bridge. She heard the sounds of water around her and followed it to the edge, a three-foot concrete railing between her and the river.

Just a few inches, she thought, her mind numb. She could jump; no one was around to pull her out. Her body would float downstream and probably wash up on shore. Some jogger would find her in the morning and call the police. Then they would call Leta and she would deny she had a sister and life would go on for everyone, except her. But that would be okay, because she would finally have peace.

Twelve

"THIS WAY PLEASE."

Noah followed behind Alma as the hostess led the way to their table. She waited until they were seated before advising them their server would be by shortly. He smiled politely and thanked her as she walked away. Alma, on the other hand, excused herself to the restroom, which was fine, considering the painful drive they had just endured. Not one word was spoken after she told him what restaurant to go to—not from her and not from him. He simply drove to their destination stewing in the fact that Alma had led him on and used him.

She did say dinner only, he reminded himself.

Shut up.

Noah's pocket started vibrating. His phone was ringing again. With a sigh of disgust, Noah pulled it out and looked at the number. It was Cass'. He knew why she was calling, but he didn't feel like talking to her right now and explaining where he had been or why he hadn't returned. She would beg for details and that would be a hard conversation to have, especially since he had nothing to tell—not now and not tomorrow, when he'd pick up his personal items from the bookstore after being fired in person. Ten years down the drain and for what?

The phone stopped vibrating and within a minute a voicemail notification popped up on the screen. Before Noah could retrieve it, his phone vibrated again. This time it was Bill. Like Cass, he let the phone go unanswered. Sure enough he received another voicemail notification. He had a good idea of the message Bill left him, so Noah didn't even bother. He simply stuck it back in his pocket, as Alma returned to the table. He glanced at her briefly, before picking up his menu and pretending to browse through it. He couldn't help the disappointment that invaded his heart and wasn't sure he could sit through the next hour or so with her.

"Their crab cakes here are awesome...for a bar," Alma said.

Noah nodded, but said nothing. Instead he glared at the menu in front of him, wishing there were pictures instead of words so he could focus his sights on something other than her.

Oh, grow up. Stop acting so childish.

I'm not.

What would you call it then?

Uh...

Their waiter appeared and set a plate of bread in front of them. After greeting them, he ran through the list of specials for the night and offered to return if neither of them was ready to order. Noah was going to ask for a few extra minutes when Alma spoke up, a smile on her face and a twinkle in her eye.

"I'll have the crab cakes with a glass of red wine. Will that work?"

Noah frowned. What was she doing? Flirting with the waiter?

"Yes, ma'am. And you, sir?"

Noah quickly looked back down, as though he had been caught doing something wrong. He scanned the menu but again, there were no pictures so he couldn't pick something, anything. Why didn't he just ask for more time?

Because you're a guy.

That's stupid.

Plus, you don't know how to go after what you want.

She said she didn't want anything besides dinner.

Why'd she kiss you then?

I don't know.

Maybe you should ask. Or are you just going to sit back and do nothing, like always?

I don't do that.

Yeah? What about Sage?

Can we just focus on dinner? My dinner?

"Uh, I'll have the same," Noah said finally. Then added, "Get me a beer though."

"Absolutely," the waiter replied. He picked up the menus and walked away.

"I was going to say, you don't look like a red wine type of guy," Alma commented.

She was flirting with the waiter and now she wanted to carry on a conversation with him as though this were normal? Obviously, she was more…promiscuous than him. He couldn't hold it against her, could he?

If I'm paying for dinner, yeah!

That's sexist.

Shut up!

"It's not my thing," he muttered, annoyed with his thoughts.

"Well, to each his own, right?" she stated, then picked up the small loaf of bread in front of her and cut into it. Then she asked about his job. Last time a girl inquired about his employment, it ended badly. His anger level rose with each question she posed. He needed a distraction, something to take his mind off the current state of affairs. He picked up the other half of the loaf and transferred it to his plate. He should've been hungry—he hadn't eaten anything since breakfast—but his appetite was gone. And he knew why.

Regardless of what Alma had said, there had to be something between them.

Summoning up some courage, Noah asked again about the kiss. She deflected. Then the waiter returned with their drinks. An inopportune interruption, Noah thought; and from the way she proceeded to flirt with him, an especially infuriating one.

"Okay, so what was that about?" Noah questioned, not bothering to hide the disdain in his voice. When she dismissed his question, he argued back, bringing up all the guys she had flirted with just in the few hours she was with him. He was flustered and it showed in his words and the way they came out in such a hurry. Noah hadn't intended to say everything he did, but it all came out—and in one breath.

He didn't get the response he wanted though.

"I told you, it was nothing, okay? Don't read into this."

"Read into what?" he demanded in exasperation.

"Just because I said yes to dinner doesn't mean there's something between us. Because this? This is just dinner. This is me being hungry and taking advantage of a guy who wants to go out with me. I never promised you anything more than that. In fact, I've had a busy enough day without you in it."

"I'm the one who drove you everywhere!" he retorted. "If it wasn't for me, you'd still be at the boutique, dress shopping."

"Screw you!"

"Yeah, you did that already too. Or at least you tried."

Alma's mouth fell open, but nothing came out. She wanted to fight, he could tell; to keep arguing, to tell him off, but words seemed to fail her. Noah wanted to battle as well but seeing the uneasiness in her countenance gave him pause. All day, she had been confident, sure in her actions. From the kiss to the way she invited herself into his car and his life, Alma was unapologetic. She reared life in and forced it to bend its will to hers. Yet here she was, uncertain and insecure...mostly. Noah wouldn't dare call her that to her face, but in that moment, he saw a vulnerability in her that begged for protection from all the things she was perhaps covering with the air of confidence.

Noah's will to argue instantly left him. He had allowed his anger to get the best of him and for that he was ashamed, especially when he noticed the other diners staring at them. Looking to remedy the situation he had created, Noah decided to turn the conversation around.

"So…," he began, turning his gaze back to Alma. "Why did you wear the dress out?" he asked, changing his tone so that it reflected not the anger he had let out earlier, but the compassion he felt for her. The question though seemed to take her by surprise. He repeated it, then watched as she struggled to respond. Finally, she said, "I don't know. I really liked the dress and I wanted to wear it today."

"It looks good on you," he said quietly. He meant it.

Alma appeared to relax. Then their small world turned upside down when a waitress hastily approached their table and threw a glass of ice water in Alma's face. Noah was slow to react, especially when the crazed woman started shouting at Alma, calling her names and threatening to call the police. He didn't understand what was happening, but when he saw the woman lunge at Alma again, he rushed to her side. Then a male voice interrupted them and drew their attention to him. Both women turned towards the handsome man in a chef's uniform hurrying to the waitress' side. He wrapped his arms around the waitress and pulled her away from the table. He encouraged her, speaking tenderly to her. But he did not once make eye contact with Alma, who seemed devastated by the lack of attention. She reached for him as he walked away, but he paid her no mind.

Alma looked around her, eyes glistening with tears. Noah wanted to comfort her, to make her feel better but he didn't know where to begin.

"Alma?" he said, gently.

It was too late though: she grabbed her purse, ran towards the door and disappeared once again. Noah watched her go, his body frozen in place just as before. Only when she had cleared the door did his mind kick into gear and scream at him to follow her.

Or you'll never see her again. You got lucky this morning. You might not be so lucky later.

"Alma!"

Noah started after her, but a waiter grabbed his arm.

"Whoa, buddy," the man said. "You still need to pay for your drinks."

"Are you kidding?" Noah asked, exasperated. "After what *your* waitress did, the least you can do is skip the bill."

"That's not how it works. Besides, *your* girlfriend is not supposed to be here."

Noah thought to argue, to have him expound on that last point, but he knew if he didn't leave soon, Alma would be lost to him. He reached into his wallet and threw some money on the table, enough to cover the drinks.

"Classy joint you have here," he remarked with sarcasm, then went after Alma.

Thirteen

NOAH RAN OUTSIDE AND looked around him. The street was moderately busy with the nighttime crowd, people coming and going, and standing and walking. Noah had to push his way through them. He hurried down the sidewalk towards the river, peering into businesses and scanning faces. Alma was nowhere to be found though. It seemed she had disappeared into thin air. Just like earlier. But she had only a slight lead on him. Where did she go?

"Alma!"

This is ridiculous! he thought to himself. *She's gone.*

Still Noah kept going. He couldn't explain it, but he had to find Alma. Maybe because he needed to justify his day; or because he was genuinely concerned for her; or maybe he was hoping she would reconsider seeing him again.

Were you not paying attention in the restaurant? The girl's got issues and you don't need to get in the middle of them. If you were smart, you'd run the other way.

But he didn't. He crossed the street and ran into the park. A fool's errand, at best; but it seemed the only logical location for Alma to run. He ran along the trail, following the contours of the river. Darkness had fallen upon them, so Noah had to depend on the street lights above to see where he was going. He continued, looking for Alma's dress, her dark hair, her shapely form. All he saw though were joggers, dog-walkers and families out for an evening stroll. He wanted to believe he was close to finding Alma, that she was around the next bend, or sitting on a nearby bench, but when the crowds thinned and the trail wound further into the park, Noah knew he had lost her.

He stopped walking, his breath heavy in his chest. What was he thinking? Maybe it was a good thing he didn't catch her. Alma was out of his league, even with the relationship trouble she had. His best qualities were his laziness and lack of ambition; and neither contributed to a healthy relationship, or so Sage said. Sadly, she was right.

Still struggling to get his breath back, Noah stepped off the trail and leaned back against a tree, his hands resting on his knees. He really needed to exercise more, but like everything else, he was too *content* to do so. His life basically consisted of work and not much else. He played video games, went shopping for basic necessities and hung out with the few friends he had, but nothing more than that. His life was boring. Alma had offered him the first sense of fun in a long time.

Noah sighed. Did he continue looking for her or call it a night? He looked around him. There was a street light nearby, giving everything a dim, soft glow. Beyond it, the trail, a bridge, trees and leaves, and more trees and more leaves. It was hopeless.

Then, as he stood upright, Noah saw a figure sitting on the bridge's ledge. He couldn't tell who or what it was, but in his heart, he felt it was Alma. He stepped back onto the trail and made his way to the bridge. The closer he got, the more confident he became. He couldn't see her face as her back was to him, but he knew. It wasn't until he was behind her that he saw it was indeed Alma.

Noah stopped and cleared his throat.

"Don't jump," he quipped.

She glanced at him briefly, before returning her gaze to the water. Something about her stance, her disposition told him she was still distraught. Noah ventured closer, leaning against the railing beside her. He wasn't good at talking, and awkwardly waited for her to say something (since girls usually did that kind of thing first), but Alma said nothing. She didn't even look at him.

What did guys do in this situation? How was he supposed to fix something like this? Wait? Talk? Maybe hold her?

Too soon, his mind yelled.

Dude, she was going to give you a blow job earlier.

Oh, yeah.

"I'm a pretty good listener if you want to talk," he finally said. But again, she didn't respond. Out of practice, or rather, inexperienced when it came to the fairer sex, Noah moved closer to her and was ready to place his arm around her shoulder, when she suddenly twisted her body so that she was facing him.

"Do I look like a jumper?" she asked.

Not the 'something' Noah was expecting.

"A jumper?"

"Do I look like the type of person that, if I decided to commit suicide, I would choose jumping?"

Noah was baffled by the question, but attempted to answer it, nonetheless.

"No. I don't think so."

"What would you say I look like?"

Noah studied her face, but not for an answer. Alma didn't look distressed, but neither was she the flighty, carefree person he had met earlier. Instead, her tone was cynical, and she was once again guarded.

"I guess you look more of a pill-swallower," he responded.

Alma guffawed, then stated, "I don't think that's a word."

"Sure, it is, if you do that kind of thing."

"Well," she began, pulling her skirt up and throwing her leg over the side of the railing, so that she was straddling it. "If you're a woman, the statistics are higher that you'll kill yourself by overdosing rather than by committing violence against yourself. So that rules out jumping. Though I once saw a photo, this woman jumped off a skyscraper sixty or seventy years ago and landed on a car below, denting the hood of it. But she didn't explode into pieces or get mangled up, the way they do in movies. Instead, she was laid out across the vehicle, her legs crossed daintily and her hand holding the string of pearls hanging around her neck." Alma mimicked her words as she spoke. "She had the most serene expression on her face. The photograph eventually became known as the 'Beautiful Suicide.'" Alma paused and looked down at her hands, resting open on her lap. She touched her thumb to each fingertip, then closed her hands into fists. She offered an apologetic grin and made eye contact. "Morbid conversation, huh?"

Noah shrugged his shoulders.

"I don't know. I suppose everyone has thought about death at one point or another."

"What would you do? How would you die?"

"Ideally? In my sleep. I am not good with blood or drowning or exploding or anything that causes even the minutest pain."

Alma laughed at him.

"Low threshold, huh?"

"Stubbing my toe is traumatic. And don't even get me started on paper cuts."

She laughed again, her smile lighting up her beautiful face. Noah wanted to touch her, to cup her cheek in his hand, to kiss her. But even though she was free with her emotions, he was not. He could admit he liked her and wanted to see more of her—figuratively and literally—but there was a niggling fear that kept him from doing so. What if she only kissed him because she was bored? Or because he was convenient? She did say she was only having dinner with him because she was hungry.

Why does any of that matter? Even if you weren't afraid, you wouldn't kiss her.

I'm a gentleman.

You're a coward.

Shut up. She'd get to know me and…

Fourteen

ALMA STOPPED AS THEY reached the second-floor landing and removed her heels.

"Sorry," Noah stated. "The elevator is kinda iffy. It was working this morning."

Grocery bags in hand, he stood on the step above her, waiting patiently. He bore such a pitiful expression; Alma didn't have the heart to tell him 'this' was not what she had in mind when she said camping. They had stopped and picked up supplies, including hotdogs, marshmallows, graham crackers and chocolate, but when they drove to his apartment building to 'camp', Alma's excitement waned. This was the last thing she expected from the trepid shopkeeper. Still, she was intrigued: he kept telling her she would enjoy the view.

Now barefoot, Alma shoved her shoes into her purse, slung it over her shoulder and resumed her pace. She took Noah's hand and ascended the stairs with him. It was probably silly that she continued to hold onto him, but she needed to feel him in her hands. She couldn't explain it, but there was something comforting about his presence and she liked having him near. It probably sent the wrong message, but if he was willing to indulge her for the night, then she was going to take what she could get.

When they reached the fourth floor, Noah said, "Just three more flights." He was out of breath.

"I thought you said your apartment is on the fourth floor," Alma asked, breathless herself.

"It is. We're going to the roof, though," he replied and continued climbing.

The thought of taking another step was enough to make Alma throw up. She wasn't very athletic (hence the rounder figure) and often relied on elevators and escalators to ease the hardship of physical activity.

Too winded to make conversation, both of them continued going until they arrived at the seventh-floor landing and a door marked 'Roof'. Noah let go of her hand and unlocked the door. He stepped aside to give her passage. Alma walked by him and was suddenly surrounded by palm leaves of all sorts. The greenery was lush and spread out to create a wholly different atmosphere. Alma pushed through it to find a colorful blanket tented up over them. Several wooden lawn chairs surrounded a fire pit, while Christmas lights lit up the area. Beyond it were the lights and sounds of the city, set against the backdrop of a beautiful night sky. Few stars were visible, but to Alma, it didn't matter. The setting was perfect. It was more than she could have asked for.

"This is awesome," Alma exclaimed, as she moved past the chairs and fire pit to the brick railing surrounding the roof. She leaned forward as far as she could and stared at the street scene below. She had noted the restaurants and clubs that filled the street when they drove in but looking at them now from above made it seem like a different world. It made her feel…bigger.

"You're not going to jump, are you?" Noah said.

Alma smiled as she turned around towards him. He had stopped at the fire pit and set the bags on one of the chairs.

"Don't worry; I don't plan on going out like that," she assured him.

"Okay, good. Because my roof access would probably be revoked if you did that," he said, tongue-in-cheek.

Alma laughed.

"Just kidding," he added. "I'll start the fire."

Noah emptied out the bags and added kindling to the pit.

"Whose set up is this?" she asked.

"Hedy, the landlord's daughter. She's an art student, comes up here to paint."

"The artsy-fartsy type, huh?" Alma asked.

"I guess."

He added wood and doused it with starter fluid. Then he lit a match and the fire roared to life. Alma watched as Noah opened a package of hotdogs and impaled them on bamboo skewers. He followed suit with the marshmallows. He set everything aside on one of the chairs, along with the paper plates, buns and condiments, and waited for the fire to settle. Content everything was as it should be, Noah took a seat and grabbed a couple of beers from one of the bags. Alma took it as her cue that she should join him and walked over to the lawn chairs. She seated herself next to him and accepted the beer when he handed it to her. He had offered to purchase wine earlier, but she had turned him down, wishing to make his evening easier than she had made his day.

"Is she sweet on you?" Alma asked as she leaned back and brought her feet up on the chair. She dropped her purse on the floor beside her and turned to Noah in time to see him blush.

"I don't think so."

"So, everybody in the building can come

up here?"

"Uh…no."

"Then she must like you to let you come up here to her sanctuary, don't you think?"

"No. I'm sure…no; I've seen her with other guys. No."

Noah took a swig of his beer and glanced at everything else, except her. He was definitely uncomfortable, not just with the conversation but with the prospect of unwanted female attention. Not unlike when they were at the mission earlier. Granted, she might have come on a tad strong, but he seemed uneasy, if not inexperienced, in the areas of romance and sex.

"Are you a virgin?" she asked suddenly.

Noah choked on his drink. Alma might have laughed if she wasn't so intrigued. She had slept with a good number of men and women, but none were virgins. She waited for Noah to stop coughing before she continued. "You are, aren't you? You're a virgin!" It made sense now; if he was unexperienced, then her actions would have frightened him.

"What? No!" he exclaimed, dismissing her comment as if it were no longer obvious.

"Look, it's okay. There's nothing wrong with that," she insisted. "Though it does explain why you turned me down."

Alma slid to the edge of the chair, her

knees brushing his. She reached out to touch him, but Noah moved away from her.

"You caught me off guard, that's all," he said quickly, then stood up. He picked up the skewers and held them over the fire, avoiding Alma's gaze. She smiled. She meant what she said, it was okay that he was still 'innocent' and 'pure'. It was a reflection of his personality and only added to his charm.

Of course, there was nothing wrong with sex either; as far as she was concerned, every responsible adult should know the joys of it. Noah proved to be responsible. It was her duty then to introduce him to that pleasure.

Alma rose to her feet and approached Noah with quiet steps. He eyed her with a sideways glance, then returned his gaze to the hot dogs. She took the skewers from his hand and laid them back on a paper plate. Then she turned back to him and took his hand in hers. She brought her hand up to his cheek and gently caressed it with her thumb. Alma let go of his hand and placed her hand on his other cheek, cupping his face. He watched her with curiosity, but also shame, something Alma couldn't understand, but vowed to fix.

"Let's finish what we started earlier then and remedy this little problem of yours."

Up on her tip-toes, Alma stood ready to kiss him, when she felt his hands rest on hers.

His expression was apologetic, his actions hesitant.

"Can I ask you something?"

And here we go again.

"I told you already," Alma said, as she pulled her hands out of his, disappointed. "I don't want to talk about that kiss—"

"No, not that," he replied quickly, though she wasn't completely convinced the question wouldn't worm itself into their conversation again. "It's about the restaurant."

Alma let out a noisy breath, backed away from him and dropped into her chair. She didn't want to talk, she wanted to have sex. She wanted to step away from the world for the next hour or so and just live in the moment where pleasure was all she could feel. But Noah was being obstinate. She never had to work so hard to get a guy.

"No," she pouted.

She expected an argument, but Noah didn't give her one. "Okay" was all he said and resumed cooking the hotdogs. He didn't appear to be upset; he simply focused on the fire pit—stroking the wood, cooking the hot dogs, preparing the marshmallows. He seemed unperturbed by her denial, which left her on the defensive. Alma wasn't sure why she felt the need to justify herself to him, but she did.

"It's a long story I don't want to rehash, ancient history," she stated, matter-of-factly. She crossed her arms over her chest, drew her knees up and dared him to pry.

But he didn't.

"Okay."

Noah glanced at her briefly before running another marshmallow through with a bamboo stick. It was like he was mocking her.

"That girl, she was just running off at the mouth, putting my business out there. No, I shouldn't have been there, but it's wasn't like that. I don't stalk exes."

This time, Noah smiled mischievously and quipped, "Just bookstore clerks?"

"Haha," Alma dryly remarked, though she had to admit it was a good comeback. She didn't say anything else for a moment. She really did hate to relive it and she had done that enough in the past year. Alma let her arms drop to her lap. Her hands ached for a moment, her wrists especially. She rubbed them and looked elsewhere, willing herself to forget. If she could make it through the next couple of hours without having that episode of her life hanging over her head, then she could end the night in peace.

Suddenly Noah was at her side. He dropped in the empty space beside her and offered her a hotdog bun. Alma accepted it curiously, holding it out as he placed the skewered meat inside it.

"Everybody has a bad break up at some point in their lives," Noah said, looking softly at her. "My last girlfriend, really my only girlfriend, was pretty and smart. But I guess I wasn't ambitious enough for her, so she moved on. *Then* she told me. *Then* we broke up."

Alma frowned and spat out, "Bitch," without thinking twice.

Noah chuckled.

"Nah, she was right."

"No, she should have been woman enough to tell you she was unsatisfied. Only a bitch does that kind of thing," Alma stated vehemently. He looked surprised, perhaps at the tone she had taken. Regardless, she was not going to back down. "Whatever. Hopefully you found someone better," Alma added and bit into her dinner.

"I found you."

Noah sounded hopeful...which crushed Alma. She started to interrupt, to break his heart, but he continued. "Alma, I want you. You have no idea what you do to me..."

"Then why do you keep pushing me away? I'm offering myself to you—"

"But we've only known each other a few

hours—"

"And…?"

"And… you don't think that's moving fast?"

"No."

He stared at her and sighed, as if the words he wanted to say were being held hostage in his mouth.

"Why…why do you do that?"

"Do what?"

"You know," he said, gesturing at her with his hands. "With Glen and Finn and…guys."

"You mean sex?" she asked, confused at his naivety, but also amused. "What's wrong with that?"

"Nothing," he replied shrugging his shoulders and leaning back. "I guess. I know I'm inexperienced and maybe I'm just old-fashioned or really naïve; I just figured there should be something between us, like a future or something. At the very least, we should know each other before we do 'the deed'."

"No one says that anymore."

"Well, whatever then."

Their argument, this time, wasn't heated, but intellectual, if it could be described as such. Alma was trying to understand him as much as he was trying to comprehend her point of view. To be honest, though, the whole conversation was unnecessary. What was wrong with stripping down and enjoying the time they had left together.

"Seriously, what's there to know?" she asked with a sigh. "I thought someone in *your position* would be ready and willing to lose his virginity to someone as hot and sexy as me."

Noah smiled.

"I don't know. I just want it to mean more than 'just sex'."

She gazed at him thoughtfully, never guessing him to be the sentimental type.

"There's a lot to be said for 'just sex'," she said.

"What happens in the morning, though?" he asked.

She sighed.

"Noah, I can't give you what you want. I'm bad news. You'll regret the day you met me."

"You said that earlier."

"And I meant it."

"I don't agree," he said then stood to his feet, his disposition different. "Come on, let's make some s'mores."

Fifteen

NOAH WORKED QUIETLY AS HE opened the graham crackers and chocolate. He tried to hide his disappointment following Alma's rejection. Or rather his rejection of her, which was crazy and stupid. What man, handed a sure thing, said no? Was he crazy? Was there something wrong with him? Noah couldn't say for sure, but the whole thing seemed so cheap and…slutty for someone like her.

So now she's a slut?

No! Of course, not!

He wasn't trying to imply that she was a whore or anything for sleeping with anyone on the first date. Or for sleeping around for the matter.

You don't know that for sure.

Yeah, I think I do.

Okay, so what if you think you do. Alma is unlike anyone you've ever met.

Yes, she is.

So, you need to take her up on that offer. There's nothing wrong with sex. Get back over there. Tell her you're ready.

And then what?

You screw, idiot. Bang, shag, fornicate. Get.

It. On. Get it?

Noah really wanted to. He really did. There was something about her that had him so intoxicated. But if she had her way, he'd never see her again after tonight. Certainly, sex with her would leave him with the most pleasant of memories to remember her by, especially for his first time. But he wanted more. Maybe he was just infatuated, but he wanted to know her, to know what made her tick. He wanted to hang out with her, to see her smile, to make her smile. He wanted to kiss her and see her naked again; but more than all that, he wanted her to like him, the way he liked her. He wanted what he was feeling to be reciprocated to him. A tad immature for someone his age, but where the heart was concerned, maturity wasn't always an option.

Hey, you should put that on a fortune cookie, or have someone quote you.

Noah ignored his last thought and gathered the crackers and chocolate. He set them on a plate, then grabbed the skewed marshmallows and sat back down on the chair beside Alma. She was quiet now, no longer amorous, but watching him with sad eyes. With minimal eye contact, Noah handed her a skewer, a couple of crackers and half a bar of chocolate.

"Half is the usual amount," he told her. "But you can use less, especially if you're lactose intolerant. Or you can use a semi-sweet chocolate, or whatever you prefer."

"This is fine," she said. Then she followed his lead as he sandwiched the chocolate between the crackers and moved closer to the fire.

"You don't want to scorch it, just brown it," Noah said, and proceeded to show her. Alma did as he did and they sat quietly together, toasting their marshmallows. Except for the sexual tension between them, the atmosphere was nice. The Christmas lights offered a festive appearance, while the dark of the roof gave the impression of them being miles away from everyone.

"When I was little," Alma began, watching her marshmallow intently, "It was just me, and my sister and my *mami*; and we didn't have a whole lot, so we would improvise. If we told *Mami* we wanted to go camping, she would set up a tent with blankets and chairs in the living room and we would eat marshmallows."

Noah smiled, trying to imagine a younger Alma doing as she described.

"Or if we wanted to go hiking, we would spend the day traipsing through the park and eating all the junk food she could afford. *Mi abuela* would have a fit when she found out, but *Mami* would just tell her we were kids and we needed fun."

Alma became quiet again, keeping her head down as she turned her marshmallow around to toast the other side. Noah usually wasn't one to carry a conversation, so the silence quickly became awkward.

"She sounds like a great mom," he commented, to fill the space.

"She was," Alma said simply. "She died when I was five."

Noah cringed. *Good going*, he chastised himself.

"Sorry," he said.

"It's fine. I don't remember her as much as I'd like to, but stuff like that stands out."

"How did she pass?"

"She killed herself," she relied, matter-of-factly.

Noah mentally kicked himself for asking. Alma smiled though, a soft, understanding grin.

"Conversation killer, huh?" she said, meeting Noah's gaze as she spoke. "It's okay. Ancient history. She was a pill-swallower. Overdosed. We went to live with my grandmother after that."

Noah looked away and took in a deep breath, unsure of what to say or if he should say anything at all. She said it herself, it was a conversation killer and no one in their right mind could follow that up with anything worthwhile. Even if he apologized and offered her his sympathy, he would still be about twenty years too late.

"So how does this work?" Alma asked, her tone light and undisturbed by her family history.

Noah looked up at her to see what she was talking about. In one hand she had her browned marshmallow and in the other, the graham cracker/chocolate sandwich. He shook himself out of his thoughts.

"Right."

Noah set his food down on the chair beside him and moved towards Alma. His knees accidentally bumped hers, causing his heart to race at the contact. He bit his lip and reminded himself that he had turned Alma down because he apparently had some higher standard that most guys did not which was causing him to sleep alone tonight.

His little speech didn't help but was complicated by the innocent expression on Alma's face, as if she had no idea what to do next. Noah knew better than to feed into her wiles, but he so desperately wanted to touch her, to put his arm around her and feel her skin. He would not though. He would help her assemble this seemingly difficult treat, then he would return to his chair.

Noah started to help Alma but found his position awkward. He didn't want to reach over her, and he didn't want to touch her food. He could simply tell her to sandwich the marshmallow between the crackers and chocolate, but Alma's expression begged for his personal attention in the matter.

With a sigh, Noah changed seats, placing himself behind Alma. She watched him with amusement, holding the foods in her hands, waiting for his assistance. Reaching his arms on either side of her, he gently touched the outside of her hands, cupping them in his. They were soft and warm against his skin. He inhaled deeply, closing his eyes, and took in her essence.

This is stupid, he thought to himself. *She is more than capable of following instructions.*

Yeah, well, those aren't the instructions she wants. Or the ones you want either…

Noah realized then it was happening again: his male member was thinking for himself, imagining the lovely angel beside him in all her natural beauty. Noah could feel his face warm. Then cool, as a light, tingly breeze drifted into his face. He opened his eyes to see Alma blowing gently on him. When she saw his eyes had opened, she smiled knowingly, then laughed.

Apparently, she did know the affect she had on him.

Embarrassed, Noah withdrew his arms and started to pull away from her, but she quickly gathered her food in one hand and with the other, squeezed his knee.

"Don't. I was playing. I'll stop. Just stay with me. I'll stop."

Noah could hear the sincerity in her voice and relaxed his posture. He leaned back against the chair as Alma watched him carefully; once she was assured he wasn't leaving her side, she sat back against him and made herself comfortable. It didn't help Noah's little 'problem', but he certainly didn't mind. He was about to relax when Alma sprung up quickly to grab his food, handed it to him, then leaned back once again. Seemingly happy, she pulled her feet up on the chair and dug into her food. Noah heard the crunch of the cracker and watched as the melted marshmallow seeped out of the sides. Alma tried to catch the excess, but failed, her fingers and mouth covered in the sticky goo. He couldn't help but smile at her.

"Oh my God, this is so good," she squealed.

"You've really never had s'more's before?" Noah asked in disbelief.

Alma nodded as she took another bite.

"My grandmother always viewed this as white people food and we didn't do too much of that."

"White people food?

"Yeah, you know, junk food? Deep friend stuff? Snack foods that are totally unhealthy for you? Anything that's not *arroz y frijoles*."

Noah had never thought of it that way, but he had to admit she was right.

"Your grandmother would not be very happy with you now," he quipped as he made his s'more.

"She died a few years ago."

He stopped what he was doing and groaned.

"I'm just batting zero, aren't I?"

Alma laughed, then finished up her s'more.

"I want more," she said and jumped up. Noah observed her quietly, ignoring his own food as she prepared more for both of them. She roasted the marshmallows and told him about the remaining family she had: her sister Leta and brother-in-law Owen, parents to eight-year-old Zoey, who technically was seven, but would be celebrating a birthday this coming Saturday, and whose favorite animal was a hummingbird, just like her aunt. Alma doted mostly on her niece, smiling as she spoke. Noah wondered how she could cycle from one topic to another so quickly, but when she sat back, comfortably nestled between his legs, a plate of food for them, he let the questions slip away. In between bites of s'mores, she asked him about his job and his family; and in between bites of hotdog, Noah answered her. She wasn't so forthcoming when he asked about any job prospects, but she didn't shut down like she did earlier in the day. She went back for thirds. Noah had eaten his fill though and simply watched her. Alma had a healthy appetite—for food and for life—and he really liked that.

"I have to admit," Alma stated as she cuddled up next to him again, another plate of s'mores in her hands. "I was a little concerned when you brought me here, but I was wrong. This is by-far the best camping trip I've ever been on."

"I figured it was the best we could do on short notice," Noah replied. Then before he could stop himself, he added, "We could plan for the real thing for a later date." He cringed, not wanting to rehash any of their earlier conversation. One-time rejection was enough for him. "Or whatever," he said dismissively in an attempt to salvage their exchange.

Alma stared out into the night sky and

ate her food. She didn't answer him, or acknowledge his last comment, leaving Noah to wonder what was going on in her head. After a while, she finished up and placed her plate on the ground. Then, she curled up next to him and rested her head on his chest.

"You're a really nice guy, Noah."

Her voice was so small.

He started to tell her what he thought of her as well, but she brought her hand to his lips and stopped him.

"Just say thank you, okay?"

With no room to object, Noah nodded, and did as she asked.

"Thank you."

She relaxed then, placing her arm around him, and closing her eyes. Noah's arms naturally fell around her and he pulled her in to a tight embrace. Alma didn't seem to mind; in fact, she drew closer to him until their bodies were seemingly one. He ran his hand over her exposed arm slowly, enjoying the feel of her skin, of her tattoo and raised ink. He closed his eyes and imagined the leaves and vines he had, since that morning, come to appreciate. It was a part of her, and he liked the full package.

One of the tattoos felt wrong, though: a long, thick line amidst the fine, curly strokes. He didn't remember that. Noah opened his eyes. He thought to sit up and look at it, but he didn't want to disturb Alma whose breathing had become low and steady. She was drifting into sleep, something he should be doing. Noah let his hand rest on her arm and as he drifted off, he didn't give too much thought to what the next day might bring. He only hoped it was good.

Sixteen

THE NIGHT AIR WAS CHILLY, BUT between the fire pit and the heat from Noah's body, Alma felt warm. She also felt right, as if time had stopped and this moment existed simply for her enjoyment.

You should just stay with him here forever.

I can't.

He's different from the others.

I would only end up hurting him.

She could tell from Noah's steady breathing that he was asleep. In fact, he was snoring, though just slightly. He was experiencing a well-deserved rest after the day she put him through.

Alma wasn't done though. She should have left before when she finished eating, but she couldn't imagine leaving his side. Being with him offered her a peace she couldn't get otherwise, and this was appealing enough to make her reconsider her plans.

No, we've gotta go before it comes back.

Alma lifted her head and peeked at Noah. His eyes were shut tight, his mouth slightly ajar. It had been about an hour since they had settled in, but she had no way of knowing if he was a light sleeper or a heavy one. It was time to find out.

Withdrawing her arm from around Noah, Alma placed it beneath her and pushed up slowly. He stirred but didn't wake. Alma continued until she was up on all fours. Then she sat beside him. He turned his head to the side, away from her, still asleep. Outside of the city, only the sound of Noah's snoring could be heard.

A heavy sleeper then.

Alma let out the breath she had been holding and took a minute to collect her thoughts. This was the moment she had been waiting for, the one she had spent her day getting ready for. It was finally here. Then she remembered the list. Her movements slow and careful, Alma edged off the chair and slipped onto the cold floor. She reached under the chair and snatched the handles of her purse, pulling it towards her with calculated movements. Every inch it moved sounded like a freight train barreling through a crossroad. Alma stopped, but Noah continued sleeping. So, she continued pulling. When she finally got hold of it, she found the list. It was worn and crumpled; and in this lighting, almost illegible.

Alma sighed; she should have found a clean piece of paper to use when inspiration struck, but she was afraid she might forget something, so she grabbed the first thing available to her—a scrap sheet she had used as a grocery list. Now as Alma tried to decipher her writing, she decided she should have chanced forgetting. She got her bearings, found a pen in her purse and read through it again.

Kiss Noah

Talk to Finn

Send Book La Vida

Extra whipped cream and sprinkles

Sunrise, Sunset

Go see Rosa

Present for Zoey's birthday

Bucket list

Get a dog, name it Rick

Pick up paycheck

Die happy

New dress

Donations

Do something normal

While this wasn't the most exciting bucket list, she got to say goodbye to the people who mattered to her. And she actually did get to see a sunrise and a sunset, something she often missed.

She didn't diet or budget, but today she was determined to splurge on herself and enjoy the little things, like sprinkles.

Saad and the guys accepted her donation so this one could get crossed out. They needed the money more than she did anyway.

Camping was something normal families did. This definitely got crossed off.

She would never get a dog though, and his name would never be Rick. Not that it really mattered; she'd probably kill it. She couldn't scratch this entry off the list. Or the next one—Talk to Finn. Alma failed miserably when it came to Finn. Not only did she *not* talk to him, she broke down in front of him. This wasn't the impression she wanted to leave him with, but it was too late now. She had violated the court order by going to see him. She had broken the terms of the agreement by walking into that restaurant and pretending she was normal like all the other patrons. She wasn't; and if she attempted another visit, she would end up in jail.

No, her opportunity to talk to Finn and

apologize was lost. And while Alma would've happily ended it there, there was one task she had to complete, though she was dreading it:

Call Leta

Alma could feel her heart drop into her stomach; not just figuratively, but literally. At least that's what it felt like. Everything hurt now. She loved Leta, but she hated talking to her older sister. Like the others, all Alma had to say was 'goodbye', but she knew the conversation would eventually turn into how much of a disappointment she had become. And God forbid if Leta found out Alma had tried to talk to Finn. She would kill her.

That would save me the trouble at least.

As much as she dreaded the thought, however, this was one call Alma had to make. She set the list down and got her phone out of her purse. It was on half charge, more than enough battery for Leta to chew her out a couple of times. Reluctantly, Alma dialed her sister's mobile number and waited, praying no one picked up.

The phone clicked over on the third ring. "Hello?"

A male voice. It was Owen, Leta's

husband. He stayed out of the sisters' relationship, getting only Leta's take on the matter, but that meant his opinion of Alma was undoubtedly skewed; and for that reason, Alma avoided him. Even now.

"Alma?"

His voice was groggy, as if she had woken him up. Only then did Alma consider the time. It was well past midnight, though she was unsure of the hour. She slid down further on the floor and rested her head back on the chair, no longer worried about waking Noah. He would sleep through a hurricane if one hit.

Alma heard her sister in the background asking Owen who was on the phone. Alma wanted to hang up, to hide under a rock somewhere, but she couldn't. She had come this far, she needed to finish.

"Do you know what time it is?" Now Leta was on the line and she was angry. "What is it now, Alma? What did you do?" Her tone was accusatory. "What is so necessary to say that you call here at two, almost three o'clock in the morning?"

"I…" *Say it.* "I…I'm sorry."

Leta sighed into the phone.

"Sorry for what? What did you do?"

"I didn't," Alma said, her voice low. "I just wanted to say sorry for everything I put you through."

Leta paused. Beyond the accusations, Alma knew suspicion would follow. And why not? Leta wasn't stupid. She had lived through their mother's suicide. She knew the signs to look for, if she were willing to pay attention. She wasn't always, but now she had no choice.

"Where are you?" she finally asked.

Alma ignored the question.

"Please tell Zoey I love her, okay?"

"Alma, where are you?"

"I love you," she told her sister. And despite their differences, she really did. She could only hope Leta felt the same way. "*Yo te amo,* Leta."

"Don't hang up! Wait," her sister pleaded, but Alma was done. She released the grip she had on the phone and ended the call, in spite of Leta's begging. Then she turned the phone off and set it down on the ground beside her purse. She sat up, feeling…what did she feel? Sad? Happy? No. Perhaps part of her did feel a balance of the two emotions, but more than anything, she felt relieved. She felt…complete. She had done what she set out to do, said good-bye to those she loved, and she even got a little sweetness out of the deal.

Alma turned around. Noah hadn't stirred

but continued to sleep. She got up on her knees and slowly, quietly leaned over him. She watched him for a moment, marveling in his simplicity. He really was a nice guy, she meant what she said. Alma wasn't sure why she told him as much as she did, but she appreciated the gift he had given her: a moment of comfort when it counted most.

With bated breath, Alma leaned forward and gently kissed Noah on his cheek, lingering as she enjoyed the feel of his skin beneath her lips.

"Thank you," she whispered, then rose to do the only thing left to her to do.

Seventeen

"DON'T HANG UP! WAIT," Leta pleaded, but Alma did so anyway. The phone clicked. Then silence.

"Leta, what is it?" Owen asked from his side of the bed.

Leta didn't respond but dialed her sister's number. The phone immediately went to voicemail though: Alma had turned it off. Leta tried again, hoping she was wrong, hoping maybe she called back too quickly. Like before though, the call went to voicemail.

"Leta!"

She looked up. Owen was sitting up now, his pajamas wrinkled, his hair tussled. The concern written all over his face would have been sweet if it wasn't for the current situation.

"What did she say?" she demanded.

"You know she doesn't talk to me," he replied.

"Well, did you hear anything? On the phone? In the background?"

"No. What's wrong?"

"It's Alma. Again," Leta stated, disdainfully, as if that explained everything.

She tossed the phone on the bed, threw the covers off and stood up. "I don't know what the hell she did, but I am so sick of this."

"Do you want me to go look for her?" Owen offered.

Leta shook her head and began pacing.

"No. She's not your problem."

Owen 'hmphed'. She stopped and gazed at him.

"What?"

"This!" he exclaimed. "We've been married ten years and you say this isn't my problem." He rose from the bed and walked over to her, exasperated. "I never once gave you grief about your sister or your family. I never suggested I wouldn't mind getting involved, yet you continue to push me away."

"No, I don't," Leta returned defensively.

"You're doing it now."

"Well, she's *my* sister."

"And now mine."

He chooses now to get offended? Owen had always understood when it came to her *familia*, giving her the distance, she needed to deal with Alma and her *abuela*; so to have him attack her like this now was beyond her comprehension. Did he really think he could help? Did he believe he could handle Alma better than she could? Did he, all of a sudden, know how to solve this?

"You don't know what we went through," she said, coldly.

"And whose fault is that?" His tone was just as icy as hers.

"How dare you?" she spewed. "After everything I do for you and for this family and you want to argue about what I shield you from? What I choose not to trouble you with?"

"You don't get it. This isn't about you, or what you do. This is about us. When I said, I do, I took on responsibility for you and for everything that affects you. But you are so stubborn; you think you have to control everything."

"What the hell is wrong with you? You act like this is my fault—"

"I never said that—"

"I didn't do anything wrong—"

"No one is saying that."

Owen reached for her with open arms, but Leta was not ready to be placated. She stepped away from him.

"Alma's the one who's always in trouble. She's the one who's always screwing up. While I'm the one who has to save her, I'm the one who's gotta bail her out of jail and pay for some expensive lawyer to keep her ass out of prison." Leta was yelling now. She could hear the pitch of her voice rising with every word, but she couldn't stop it. "I've done everything I can to help her and for what? To get woken up in the middle of night for this? So that my husband can attack me and tell me how much of a failure I am as a wife and mother for wanting to keep this from my family? I never asked for this. I never asked for…for…" Leta started pacing again. "…a crazy sister and a suicidal mother. I was the one taking care of everyone, making sure Alma had enough to eat and *Mami* didn't…do something stupid. I never asked for this and I'll be damned if I'm going to let it ruin the life I've made for myself!"

She was out of breath but determined. She eyed Owen with a steely gaze and dared him to argue. But all fight had gone out of him. His arms dropped to his side and he returned her gaze—but with sorrow.

I don't need your pity, she thought and crossed her arms over her chest.

Owen sighed.

"Leta, you can't control this," he said softly. "You can't control Alma."

"I know!" she yelled. "I know," she repeated, her voice lower.

"Then stop trying and just…" His voice trailed off, as if he was searching for the right words. Leta knew exactly what he was trying to say, though.

"I'm not her babysitter," she asserted.

"No, you're not," he replied, shaking his head. His cool demeanor returned. "You're her sister. Act like it."

Leta opened her mouth to argue, but Owen walked away without a second glance.

"Where are you going?" she demanded.

"The bathroom," he grumbled, as he turned the light on and shut the door.

Well, fine, she thought and returned to bed. She threw the blanket over her and shut her eyes tight, ignoring Owen when he climbed in beside her. She waited for him to embrace her and apologize, because that's what he always did. They had not once gone to bed upset with each other in the ten years of their marriage and while she didn't care to start now, Leta refused to let the matter lie. Alma was always doing this, dumping her troubles on her. This was just another one of those times. Just another one of her attention-getting episodes. Everything Alma. Because the world revolved around her and only her. Well, Leta wasn't going to fall for it. She wasn't going to give in. Not to Alma and certainly not to Owen. He would have to give her more than an apology.

He turned his back to her though and went to sleep. In a few short minutes, he was snoring. Leta was angry beyond words. She thought to wake him up, but she was bigger than that. Bigger than all of them. She would go back to sleep and show them.

But sleep evaded Leta. No matter how long she kept her eyes closed, or how hard she tried to rest, or how much she willed herself to sleep, all she could do was lay in bed and listen to the deafening silence of twilight. She was certain she would never sleep again, until Zoey woke her up.

"We're going to be late, Mommy," the little girl said.

Leta turned to the clock on her nightstand. Seven-thirty. She hadn't just slept, she *over*slept. She turned to the opposite side of the bed and saw it was empty. Owen had already left for work. She quickly jumped up out of bed, threw on some shoes and ran downstairs to the kitchen, where Zoey was waiting on her.

"You have your lunch?" she asked her daughter as she looked for her keys.

"Yes, Mommy," Zoey dutifully replied.

"And your bookbag?"

"Yes."

"And your homework?"

"Yep," Zoey said, nodding her head. Leta found her keys and grabbed her purse. She stopped and glanced at her daughter for the first time that morning. Her beautiful face was clean and rosy. Her rich brown hair was combed back and neat. Her dress was colorful and complimentary on her. Everything about her was flawless. Leta couldn't have been more blessed.

"You are perfect; you know that?" She kissed Zoey. The little girl scrunched up her face and said, "Eww, Mommy, you didn't brush your teeth."

Leta laughed. "I'll grab some gum, okay? Now, let's get you to school."

They made it there in no time but ended up near the end of the carpool line. Zoey would most definitely be late. Leta got comfortable and listened as her daughter excitedly chatted away about her upcoming birthday party. This reminded Leta she still needed to confirm the headcount with the salon. She reached into her purse to get her phone but couldn't find it.

Then she remembered Alma's phone call. Leta had forgotten about it in her hurry that morning, which meant the phone was still at home. Panic set in. Leta looked around her: several cars had pulled up behind her, trapping her into the carpool line. Suddenly, all of Zoey's talk had Leta on the edge of her seat. She stared at the car in front of her, willing it to move, but nothing happened. She tapped her fingers on the dashboard, as her left leg began bouncing nervously on its own. She looked at the clock—seven-fifty. It had been a few hours since Alma called.

What if she did it? She tried before.

She just wants attention.

What if she succeeded this time, though and you've already gotten 'the call'?

After the events of last year, Leta cringed every time her phone rang, wondering if this would be the time she would get the call letting her know Alma had succeeded in killing herself.

You should have gone after her.

No, I would have only enabled her.

Yeah, to kill herself…just like Mami.

Leta didn't think of her mother that often because of the last time she saw her: pale, dying, a shadow of her former self. The woman had swallowed a whole bottle of prescription pills and downed it with a glass of wine. Leta was the one to find her and even though she was only ten at the time, she knew her mother was sick. Too often her moods teetered between complete exhilaration and crippling depression. When she was older, Leta would research the condition and give it a name—bipolar depression. But it was too late for her mother at that point and too late for her after she overdosed: by the time paramedics arrived at the house, she was dead. Child services were called, and both girls were taken away until their grandmother could get them. None of them spoke of that night: Alma was too young, Leta wanted to forget and their grandmother grieved until she died. But as they grew older, Alma began showing signs of the same sickness. She was becoming their mother, and that scared Leta more than she cared to admit. After all, if it was in their genetic make-up, what did it mean for her? Or for Zoey?

"Mommy!"

Leta was jarred out of her thoughts by her daughter's voice.

"What?"

"You can move forward."

She gazed at the gap in the line in front of her and quickly pulled up.

"Are you okay?" Zoey asked.

Leta sighed, wishing she had been born into another family.

"Yeah."

After dropping off her daughter at school, Leta rushed home. She left her purse in the car and ran upstairs to her bedroom. Her heart was thundering in her chest as she pulled the blankets off, searching for her phone. She could barely hear her own thoughts. Finally, she spotted the phone; she was quick to grab it, but slow to wake it, afraid of what the notifications might be. She said a prayer and hit the button.

One missed call from Alma.

Oh, thank God, she thought.

But her relief turned to dread when she listened to the voicemail.

"'You don't know me,'" the male voice began, hesitantly and audibly distraught, "'But I knew your sister...'"

Eighteen

THE DREAM WENT SOMETHING like this: Noah was at a dark, scary restaurant where giant macaroni noodles came out of the ground and started eating people. He escaped by running into the restroom. But not just any restroom; it was the kind found in hotels, with polished marble, tiny soaps and attendants with hand towels. Safe from the monsters, Noah decided to empty his bladder. But then a girl entered. She approached him and asked for directions to the restroom. Noah eyed her, distinctively thinking that she was a girl and shouldn't be in the men's restroom. So, he ran out, but he was no longer in the restaurant. He was now in an ice-cave with a polar bear, wrestling with it, which was strange, since he had never wrestled in his life. Noah was about to do a diving crossbody from a ledge in the cave, when a second bear grabbed his legs out from under him. He landed flat on his back and jerked himself awake.

It took Noah a moment to get his bearings and realize he was back on the roof of his building, sleeping on the lounge chair, with Alma in his arms. It was still dark outside, though hints of morning were beginning to break through the sky. The Christmas lights illuminated the dark corners of the roof while in front of them, the fire continued to burn, but just barely. And the bears? Well, they were tucked back into his subconscious.

Noah sucked in a deep breath. He had heard that eating late could give a person bad dreams, but never in his life did he experience such weirdness. Freud would have had a field day with him. The only nice part to waking up was the feel of Alma lying next to him. His arm was under her, cradling her body as she cuddled beside him. He turned his head towards her. His eyes were still adjusting to the dark, but he could see her face: she was sound asleep, a peaceful expression on her countenance. He smiled, contentedly.

A cool breeze blew by them, causing Noah to shudder. He pulled Alma closer to keep her warm (and him as well). Something felt wrong though. He was wet. Maybe the dream had him perspiring all over. Wrestling bears were good for that. But not when he had a beautiful woman in his arms.

Noah shifted slowly to his side, so that he was facing Alma. She didn't stir. Apparently, she was a heavy sleeper. He pulled slightly away from her and was mortified to find his shirt was soaking wet.

Mortified, he reached down and touched the cloth. It was inordinately wet. Was his dream that bad? Noah brought his hand up to his face. It looked black in the twilight. This wasn't right. He brought it to his nose. It smelled metallic.

What is this?

Frowning, he pulled his arm out from under Alma and sat up. His green shirt was stained on the left side where she slept against him. He looked down at Alma, who continued to sleep. Her arms were tucked against her chest, but her dress was discolored too.

What is…?

One of Alma's arms slipped lifelessly from the position it was in and dropped onto the empty space between them. A long, jagged line ran across her wrist, her arms stained black, just like his hand. He reached for her, but stopped before he could touch her, his mind troubled by what he was seeing: her wrist was open, and bleeding. Was this real? Or was it part of his dream? It had to be. Bears aside, this was infinitely worse than anything that could happen to him.

"Alma?" His voice was just above a whisper, as if he was afraid to wake her. But she remained motionless.

Noah found the courage to touch her

face: Alma was cold. Deathly cold.

Oh God.

"Alma!"

Panic overtook Noah. He jumped up on the chair and kneeled beside her, calling her name. He grabbed her shoulders and moved her body towards him, so that she was flat on her back. Noah laid his head onto her chest, listening for a heartbeat, but all he heard was his pulse, pounding in his ears. He willed himself to calm down and leaned in again. This time, he felt the slightest beat.

She was still alive!

Noah called her name, trying to elicit some kind of response from her. Then he saw her other wrist was also cut. She would be dead soon if he didn't do something. Frantic, Noah felt his pocket for his phone. He dialed 9-1-1.

"What is your emergency?"

"She's bleeding...she cut her wrists...," he exclaimed.

The dispatcher asked him for more information, but Noah didn't know what to say. This wasn't the way their date was supposed to end. Why would Alma do this? Why would she cut her wrists with him there?

"Sir, is she breathing?"

Of course, the situation brought up other questions: what would have happened if he hadn't woken up? If he had continued sleeping, dreaming that stupid dream? Or if he had simply gone back to sleep? Alma would have died right there in his arms.

The very thought made Noah sick.

"Sir, is she still alive?"

He fought to keep his head straight. He had to focus.

"Yes, but barely."

The dispatcher instructed him to apply pressure to Alma's wrists. Noah did as he was told. He rested the phone on his shoulder and took hold of her wrists, hoping to slow the bleeding. The majority of the blood-loss had already occurred, so he wasn't certain he was doing any good, but he continued trying to save her.

"Paramedics are about four minutes away."

Hopelessness enveloped him: they might as well have been hours away. There was nothing more he could do, except wait...and think. As the seconds ticked away, Noah held onto Alma, focusing his thoughts on her and on the elevator, praying it was working now; on Alma's family, praying he wouldn't have to call them to tell them she was dead; and on Hedy, praying she'd understand about the furniture—there was no way the blood was coming out. Noah thought about lots of things, but mostly he just prayed.

God, please don't let her die. Whatever you want, I'll do it, just don't let her die.

He wasn't particularly religious. He believed in God but never had a need for him…until now.

"They're about two minutes away, sir. Just hang on," the dispatcher encouraged.

"Thanks," Noah said. The phone slipped from where it was wedged and dropped onto the chair, next to Alma's head. He cringed. Had it fallen just a half inch to the right, it would have hit her, eliciting a cry of pain from her. Or it would have had it been any other day. But it was today, and she was unconscious and dying. Noah considered picking up the phone, remembering the dispatcher was still on the line, but he would have had to let Alma go and he wasn't going to do that. He held her closer to him, still praying, hoping God was willing to hear him and answer him.

Please save her. Please don't let her die…

Sirens sounded in the distance.

God please, I'll do anything…

They grew louder with every passing second.

Please…

Words ceased flowing he gazed at Alma, so pale, so cold and so different than the vibrant, lively woman he had spent the day with.

The sirens stopped, flashing lights illuminating the street below them.

What felt like an eternity waiting on the ambulance was now a mad rush, as the paramedics reached the roof. Noah had to release Alma to open the door to them. He pointed to where she lay and moved out of the way. The two paramedics, a man and a woman, pushed past him and immediately began attending to Alma.

"What's her name?" the woman asked Noah.

"Alma."

Noah paced in the background, trying to still his pounding heart. He couldn't stop the accusations that bombarded his already stressed mind and made him wonder if he woke up too late, if he shouldn't have seen this coming, if he made a mistake in pursuing her.

What if… what if… what if… the words were tormenting him, threatening his sanity. Noah turned away from the scene in front of him and walked to the ledge of the roof. He couldn't breathe. His hands were shaking. His mind was in pieces. What if she died? What if she didn't and she had brain damage? What if…

Noah felt like he was losing his mind.

One of the paramedics left to retrieve the gurney from the ambulance. While he was gone, Noah moved some of the furniture around to give them better access, tripping over Alma's purse in the process. He picked it up and stepped aside so they could load her onto the stretcher. Noah retrieved his phone and followed after them as they made their way downstairs. From there, they proceeded to the hospital.

Inside the ambulance, Noah watched as they continued to work on Alma. He wanted to help, to do or say something to bring her back, but found he couldn't even form a thought. He didn't know if it was numbness, or fear. Right now, it was all too much for him.

The trip was short; and when they arrived at the emergency room entrance, Noah waited as Alma was brought out first. He followed the paramedics as they wheeled her into the hospital, and past the automated doors separating them and the emergency room. A nurse stopped him from following after them, directing him instead to a waiting room. Rather than do as what was asked of him though, Noah remained where he was, suddenly overwhelmed by a sense of loss so powerful it threatened to swallow him. He had been by Alma's side this whole time, but now she was gone, and he couldn't see what was happening. Even cold and dying, she was tangible, real. He couldn't believe that in the less than twenty-fours since they met, they had gone from a kiss to this. 'Surreal' didn't even begin to describe it.

Eventually, Noah found the will to move into the waiting room, where there were people waiting. Some were trying to sleep, while others were trying to stay awake. It was obvious though all were anxious. Noah would fit right in. He walked over to a less populated seating area. Everyone there stopped what they were doing to look at him as he trudged through. Noah felt a little self-conscious about the attention, until he remembered his clothes were covered in blood. Still holding Alma's purse, he sighed, dropped into the first chair he came to and proceeded to wait.

After some time, a nurse from the front desk approached him with a clipboard and a pen.

"I need the patient information here and here," she said, lifting up the first and second page. "Insurance information goes here on page three, and I'll need a copy of the insurance card."

Noah was struck dumb for a moment.

"I don't…even know her last name," he stammered.

"Does she have family?" the nurse asked.

He remembered Alma had spoken of a sister when they were on the roof.

"Yes."

"Then you'll need to contact them."

The nurse handed Noah the clipboard before he had a chance to offer anymore arguments, then she walked off. He was suddenly overwhelmed at the thought of having to call her sister. He had no choice though. Noah set the clipboard and pen aside and opened Alma's bag. He found her phone and turned it on. There was no security password, so he was able to scroll through her contacts easily. What was the sister's name? L-something…Lora? Lina?

Leta.

He found a phone number and hit the call button, his heart pounding nervously. He prepared the message in his head and braced himself for the awkwardness.

The call went to voicemail.

Noah cleared his throat.

"You don't know me, but I knew your sister…I mean I know your sister, Alma. My name is Noah and well, she had an accident…I mean, there was an accident…Or rather she tried to…" Noah couldn't say it—

he couldn't use the word suicide. "…We're at the hospital. I'll be here."

Not even close to what he intended to say.

Noah ended the call and started to return the phone to Alma's purse, then considered her sister might call back. He closed the purse, but not before he caught sight of the scrap piece of paper he had found yesterday morning and eventually returned to Alma. He picked it up and saw that most items had been crossed off since he last looked at it. It made no sense when he first perused it, but now in context, Noah understood what it was: her suicide to-do list, everything she wanted to do before she killed herself, including kissing him. Few things were left undone, but not the main one, not the ultimate goal she had obviously worked towards:

Die happy

Nineteen

NOAH WAS LEANING IN HIS chair, elbow on the arm rest, head in his hand, when *she* walked in.

For a moment, he imagined it was Alma, with her almond-shaped face, beautiful brown eyes and tanned skin. Except this woman was taller, thinner and more refined. Even in her yoga pants and feminine t-shirt, her designer bag cradled in her arm, her name-brand walking shoes on her feet, she looked the part of the upper-crust, well above his stature. She stopped, shoulders back, chin up in the air, and looked around the waiting room with a keen eye.

It was Leta, Alma's sister.

Her gaze stopped at him and they made eye contact. There was a moment of recognition followed by absolute loathing. Noah shuddered: this wasn't going to go well.

Already uncomfortable in her presence, he sat up and rose to his feet as she walked over to him.

"Are you Noah?" she asked, stopping in front of him.

"Yeah."

The woman looked him up and down, then pointed to his shirt.

"Is that from Alma?"

Noah glanced down. The blood had dried into a dark brownish color that covered a majority of his left side. He had been self-conscious about it earlier, but now he felt embarrassed, as if the whole affair was his fault.

"Yes."

"What happened?" Her voice was stern, humorless.

"I don't know," he replied. "We fell asleep together. Next thing I know, I wake up and we're both covered in blood and her wrists are…"

Try as he could, he still couldn't say the word suicide, nor could he allude to her obvious actions. Not when the woman he had spent time with was so full of life. Noah didn't have to say anything else about it though, because Leta's eyebrow shot up—not in surprise, but contempt. He realized then what his response implied.

"No, we just met yesterday, we didn't—"

She interrupted him with a raised hand and a far more severe expression than she offered him before.

"Is that supposed to make it better? You guys are so damned superficial. You jump from bed to bed without the slightest inkling of who you're sleeping with, thinking only of yourselves."

"Wait, no—" Noah tried to argue, but Leta cut him off again, her tone sharp and biting, her words condescending and sarcastic. Her voice steadily climbed with each word, so that everyone in their corner of the waiting room was now listening to the conversation. "You're no different than the rest," she continued. "Just because you stuck around long enough to get her to the hospital doesn't make you better than them. And it sure as hell doesn't absolve you of any guilt, so don't go thinking you're a saint or something."

"But—"

"No! I don't want to hear it. In fact, I'll do you one better. You can leave now and pretend you never even met her. How's that? Just go!" Leta stated. Her eyes shifted to the chair behind him and she asked, "Are those her things?"

He nodded, not daring to voice his response. Anything he had to say was irrelevant; she would only cut him down to size then trample on whatever was left of him. Noah handed the purse and clipboard to her. Leta snatched the items from him and sat down in the seat across from him, her head high and chin forward, seemingly oblivious of his presence.

Noah sank down into his seat. He avoided looking at Leta, knowing she was angry, but he couldn't help staring. Her resemblance to Alma was uncanny, but their personalities were so different, so abrasively diverse. Then again, this was not the most auspicious event to meet under, so she could be excused for her lack of compassion. What was most troubling to him, though, was how she equated him with 'the rest'. He would be a liar if he tried to deny Alma's easy attitude towards sex, but her sister seemed to imply there were more; and that this was something that had happened before.

What the hell had he gotten himself into?

Noah's pocket started buzzing. Glad for the distraction, he pulled his phone out.

It was Bill.

Not the kind of distraction he was hoping for, but if he was calling, surely that meant he still had a job.

Noah answered his phone.

"Where are you?" Bill greeted him, his tone gruffer than usual. "First you skip out on work, then you don't show up?"

"I…" Noah was unsure of what to say, especially with Leta seated across from him. She continued ignoring him, but as loud as Bill was talking, Noah was certain she could hear the conversation. "Look, something came up; I can't talk right now—"

"Are you coming in?"

Noah took in a deep breath.

"No."

He expected an argument, but Bill simply sighed.

"I hope that whatever you're missing work for is worth your job, because you just lost it."

Then he hung up.

I hope so too, Noah thought as he pocketed his phone. Discouraged, he tried to focus on the positive things in his life. He had led a fortunate life, one that had not known tragedy. He had family members who died, but he didn't know them that well. He had been unemployed for a time, but another job presented itself before there were any serious repercussions to his finances. He had transitioned from childhood to adulthood without needing therapy. He was content, blessed and things always worked out.

But now worry was gnawing at him. What if things didn't work out this time? What if all he could do was sit back and watch his life slowly ebb into hell? What if all he got out of last night was a memory, and a horrible one at that?

You should have slept with her.

No! I should have done more. I should have

seen this coming.

Certainly, there were clues, right? Or was he so focused on her body that he missed them?

Worry did not coexist well with positivity.

Noah shifted in his seat. He looked around, hoping for something to entertain him from his thoughts, but he found nothing.

Leta's phone rang. Back straight, eyes on the wall behind Noah, she pulled her phone out of her purse and answered it. He didn't hear much of the conversation, as her voice was low, but he caught enough to get the gist.

"I don't know...still being treated...some boy...just pick up Zoey, I'll handle this."

The call ended and she resumed her stance of superiority. Noah tried to go back to the state of oblivion he had achieved before she walked in, but he was too antsy to sit. He thought to get up and walk around, but he didn't want to miss the doctor. So, he remained seated, waiting.

One-by-one, the persons waiting with them were called back to see their loved ones. Doctors and nurses arrived with news – sometimes good, sometimes bad, but it was news. Noah watched, jealousy rising up in him. How long was this going to take? He looked at the clock on the wall—minutes had turned to hours.

Ugh!

Noah considered going for coffee. Maybe he would ask Leta if she wanted one—a peace offering of sorts. He could apologize and assure her of his intentions. But she would probably take it wrong and use it as a weapon against him. Figuratively and literally.

No coffee.

There were several televisions scattered in the waiting room. Noah tried to watch but found he couldn't concentrate.

Leta completed the paperwork and brought it to the front desk.

At least she had something to occupy her time.

She returned to her seat, her face hard and beginning to show signs of agitation.

Noah could relate. Waiting was not easy.

His leg began bouncing, a nervous tick.

Finally, a doctor emerged from the double doors. He looked around and landed his sights on Noah—or rather, Noah's bloody shirt. He started towards him. Leta saw this and quickly stood up. She briskly walked up to him, meeting him halfway. Noah followed suit, provoking an annoyed expression from her.

"Are you Alma's doctor? I'm her sister.

How is she?" she stated in a flurry of words.

The doctor nodded, then advised them of Alma's condition: she had received a blood transfusion and would remain in intensive care until her vital signs were stable.

Noah breathed a sigh of relief: Alma was alive. Elated, he blurted out, "Can we see her now?"

"No," Leta responded for the doctor.

Noah stared at her, his mind unable to comprehend the simple word she had uttered. No? After all he had been through? After all he had done to make sure Alma got help? After sitting and waiting to find out if she was okay?

"I want to see her," he insisted.

Leta shook her head, returning his gaze with cold, steely eyes. He could feel his face warm.

"No," she said firmly. "She's sick. She's bipolar. Is that what you want to see? Is that why you're still here?"

"No. I just want—"

"Don't you get it? You're just another boy she played with. No different than that other one she stabbed last year. You made it out without injury; be grateful and go home. Forget you met her. She doesn't need you here complicating things."

Noah was left speechless as she finished

her argument, turned to the doctor and nodded—a quiet gesture that indicated she was ready to see her sister now, whether he was or not. The man didn't argue but directed her to follow him. They exited the waiting room, leaving Noah alone in his confusion.

Twenty

VERA PARKED IN THE LAST available spot and collected her purse, lunch bag and hobby bag. She knitted in her spare time and often shared her creations with the other nurses and patients. It was what she had become known for; and quite frankly, Vera would have it no other way.

She balanced her bags on her shoulders and exited her vehicle. It was low to the ground and with all the weight she had to balance on two bad knees, Vera was reminded once again how much she needed to lose. She tried to eat healthier, but on long days, when nothing went right, when patients died, when she was witness to the worst of humanity, Vera found it too easy to find solace in a peanut butter pie from the cafeteria or a package of cookies from the vending machine.

Oh well, she thought and took a deep breath before proceeding towards the hospital. She had been a nurse now for the better part of thirty years and loved helping others. So, when she came across a young man in a bloody shirt, sitting on a bench outside the ER, her instincts kicked in.

"Are you okay?" she asked as she approached him. He looked up at her with rich, earthy eyes—eyes filled with pain and confusion. "Have you received medical attention?"

He peered down at the shirt and stared at it as if for the first time, before shaking his head and answering, "It's not mine."

Vera understood his disposition then and inquired about the owner of the injury.

"Are they inside now?"

He nodded.

"Have you heard from the doctor yet? Are they okay?"

The man nodded again, and Vera felt some relief. But still, his expression remained forlorn. Something was obviously wrong. She glanced at her watch; she was going to be late if she lingered any longer, but she couldn't walk away, not yet. Vera removed her bags from her shoulder and placed them on the ground next to the bench. Then she took a seat beside him.

"Do you want to talk?" she asked.

He shook his head, his eyes still on his shirt.

No, most guys don't, Vera acknowledged to herself. But he didn't have to for her to help him. She'd do the talking for him.

"Are you staying? Are you waiting on

your friend, or family member?"

He shook his head again, his eyes now resting on the cars in the distance.

"Do you have a way home then?"

This time, she received no response. Vera took that to mean no. He looked so lost, her heart broke for him.

"What's your name?"

"Noah."

"Well, Noah, I'm Vera. I'm a nurse here in the Heart Center. I was actually cutting through here to minimize my walk around the campus, because obviously I'm not a big fan of physical activity, which isn't good given my profession, but I'm glad I did, since I got to meet you."

Noah gazed up at her, leery. She got that response sometimes when she talked too much.

"I don't know if you've eaten lunch—I have—but the cafeteria here makes the best peanut butter pie you've ever tasted. It'll go down great down with a cup of coffee, or tea. I'm a coffee drinker myself, but it's an acquired taste. What do you say, care to join me?"

Noah didn't answer immediately. Instead he seemed to thoughtfully consider what she was offering. Unwilling to give him a chance to turn her down, Vera used his shoulder to steady herself as she stood up, then added, "And while we're in there, we'll get you a clean shirt. Lord knows you won't stand out here if you choose to continue wearing it, but if it were me, I think inconspicuous is the way to go. You're a what? Medium? Large?"

He sighed and muttered, "Medium."

"Follow me. I'm sure we'll find something."

Vera picked up her bags and started towards the entrance. She stopped long enough to make sure he was following and proceeded towards the nurses' bay, where a couple of nurses were seated. She recognized the older one as Tina, but the younger woman was new.

"Hi Vera," Tina said.

"Hello ladies. This is my new friend, Noah. Do we have any extra blood donor t-shirts?"

The younger woman rose from her chair. "We've got a few lying around here. Let me see what I can find."

While they waited, Vera walked around the desk. She fished her wallet out of her purse, then placed her bags beneath the desk. The younger nurse returned with several shirts, folded neatly in a stack. Vera picked out the appropriate size and handed it to Noah.

"There's a restroom down the hall to your right," she said.

Noah nodded. Gripping the shirt tightly in his hand, he walked in the direction she indicated.

"Where'd you find him?" Tina asked once he disappeared down the hall.

"Outside," she replied, turning to her coworkers. "Did you see all that blood? I thought for sure he was hurt. I had to stop."

"You can't save everyone," Tina commented, obviously aware of her friend's weakness.

"I know," she replied. "But I can help. I'm a pushover when it comes to stuff like this."

"Speaking of which, did you get a chance to knit that blanket? The baby shower is this Saturday."

Vera lit up at the mention of her other favorite subject.

"Of course," she exclaimed, and was ready to dig the gift out of her hobby bag, until she saw Noah, returning from the restroom. She turned to Tina to let her know she would get it to her later, but the woman already knew. She knowingly nodded and let Vera do what she did best...outside of knitting of course.

Noah was wearing his new t-shirt, the

soiled one in his hand. He held it out uncertain of what to do with it. Vera took it and placed it in a hazardous waste bin. Then she stepped out into the hall.

"Come on, that pie is calling," she stated.

Noah dutifully followed. She led the way, expertly navigating the halls she had come to learn over the years. She continued talking as they walked towards the cafeteria.

"I'll talk to one of the paramedics, see if they can take you home. You do have a home, right?"

Noah's somber face lit up for a moment as he grinned, then muttered, "Yeah, I do."

"You have to ask these things; you know?"

They arrived at the cafeteria. It was after lunch and there were only a handful of people scattered about, drinking coffee, chatting quietly. Vera chose a table and left Noah there as she went through the food line. He didn't argue either way whether he would eat or not, so she purchased two pies and two coffees, just to be on the safe side. Balancing the tray in her hands, she walked back to the table.

"Here we go," she said, setting the dishes between them.

"Thank you," he said quietly.

Vera picked up her fork and dug into the pie.

"I'm always happy to share a slice of peanut buttery heaven with anyone willing to try it—"

Noah shook his head.

"No, I mean for the shirt…"

"Well, the shirts are free for eligible blood donors; and I would say a substantial donation was made, wouldn't you?"

Noah grinned again, though briefly. Vera took the opportunity to talk.

"I don't know what you've been through, but the last thing you need now is to keep it bottled inside. Do you have someone to talk to? A family member, a loved one, a licensed counselor, someone who will listen?" Vera asked. "I'm available too. As much effort as I put into my talking, I put the same, if not more, into listening."

"Look, I appreciate the concern," he said with a shrug of his shoulders, "But I…there's just nothing to talk about. I made a mistake, didn't listen when others tried to warn me…I should've let her walk away. Really, it's nothing. I'll be fine."

Vera studied his face. He was a handsome young man, but he looked so tired and weary. The mention of 'her' conjured up images and scenarios, drawing out the curious busybody in her, but she understood it was none of her business and she respected that. Hopefully he had someone he would be able to talk to.

"Okay," she replied. "But if you need me, I'm here."

Noah nodded and while Vera dug into her dessert, he simply picked up his fork and drew little circles into the soft, silky middle of the pie. After playing with his food for a few minutes, he finally cut a piece and ate it. His face didn't betray any emotion, whether he liked or detested it.

"Good, right?" Vera asked.

"Yes."

"I keep saying I'm going to diet and give this stuff up, but I'm a hopeless cause. I can't stay away. What's your favorite dessert?"

He sighed deeply.

"It was s'mores, but that's kind-of been ruined for me."

Twenty-One

A CONSTANT BEEPING WAS THE only sound Alma heard.

Beep, beep.

Steady and rhythmic, it broke through the haze that surrounded her and drew her back to consciousness.

Beep, beep.

She was suddenly aware that she was tangible and real—a realization of self.

Beep, beep.

She tried to move her body, but her limbs felt heavy, weak.

Beep, beep.

Little-by-little, she opened her eyes, letting them acclimate to the bright surroundings. Where was she? Everything was blurry at first, but as she focused, she realized she was in a hospital room. And the steady beeping was her heart monitor.

Beep, beep.

She was alive. She had survived the suicide attempt and she was alive.

No!

Alma never felt more disappointed in her life. She closed her eyes as feelings of frustration and discontentment washed over her. Why was this happening? She wanted to die. She wanted to end her life, to get away from the agony of her existence. But here she was, still breathing, still living. She was a failure, an absolute failure.

"So, this is what the phone call was about?"

It was Leta.

Alma opened her eyes once again. She didn't have the strength to move, only to grip the bed with her hands. She scanned the room until she found her sister, seated in a chair against the wall, opposite of the bed. Her back straight and chin out, Leta was the epitome of grace and refinement, except her countenance was stern, angry even. Alma's stomach turned and she was hit with a wave of nausea. She wanted to throw up, to heave all the contents in her stomach, but there was nothing. She wanted to disappear, but she was stuck where she was.

The monitor continued beeping.

Leta rose to her feet and walked over to the side of her bed.

"You call me in the middle of the night to tell me how much you love me, then you cut open your wrists." Her tone was severe. Alma closed her eyes, trying to shut Leta out. She lifted her right arm, resting her hand on her breast. It wasn't enough that she survived, now she had to deal with her sister's anger?

Life wasn't fair. "You are a selfish bitch; you know that? After everything we've been through, you go and do this—again."

"You…you don't know," Alma stammered defensively, her voice barely audible.

If Leta heard her, she didn't acknowledge it.

"You don't talk to me, except to make yourself feel better about killing yourself."

It seemed Leta was only there to remind her of her failures.

"You don't know," Alma repeated, a little louder.

"And that poor boy you slept with. He was sitting out there in the waiting room, covered in your blood, when I arrived. You couldn't even tell him?"

The mention of Noah was the breaking point for Alma. He was the last person she wanted to think about. Leta had no right to guilt her like this. Squeezing the tears from her eyes, Alma turned to her sister and yelled, "You don't know." Her voice was broken, dry. It pained her to yell, but she had to say it. "You don't know what it's like to know it's coming."

Leta's disposition didn't change though.

"To know what's coming?" she asked with disdain.

Before Alma could censor herself as she

had done so many times in the past, she bawled, "The depression. You don't know what it's like to know it's coming," she cried. "To know that you can't do anything to fight it. That you're eventually going to die because of it. You don't know. You lock yourself away in that perfect little world of yours and pretend that nothing and no one exists outside of Owen and Zoey, while I...I...have to deal with this. I didn't ask for this. I didn't ask to be like this. I don't sit around and think of ways to screw up your life, while you get to live a fantasy. You don't know."

"Don't you dare!" Leta warned.

"Dare what? Tell you the truth?" Alma spewed. She could feel her heart pounding now and her head was beginning to ache. Of all people, Leta should have been the one to understand.

But she didn't.

"You want the truth?" Leta returned. "I'm the one who's been holding this family together now for years. I took care of *Mami* when she was too 'sad' to get out of bed. I took care of you and made sure you ate and went to school. I'm the one who stayed up with *Abuela* when she cried with grief after *Mami* died, I'm the one who listened to Rosa fuss because she didn't know how we were going to make it. I'm the one! It was me who had to be strong and pretend like nothing was wrong. Who bailed you out of trouble countless of times. Who kept you out of the hospitals and jails. Who was there when no one else was. So don't you sit there and judge me and tell me I'm the one living a fantasy."

Leta appeared ready to explode, to hit a new level of anger and exasperation that Alma never saw before. But just as quickly as she got worked up, she stopped. The fight drained out of her and she composed herself as if she never lost control.

"I can't do this anymore, Alma. I can't lie to *myself* anymore. I can't lie to my husband or my child. I can't pretend that I don't cringe whenever I hear your name. That I don't live in fear over what you might do or if this is the day I get that phone call. I can't do it. I just can't."

Leta was too calm now, filling Alma with fear and dread.

"You're right, I'm focused on my family and I won't apologize for that. They are the one thing that this...this... thing hasn't touched or ruined, and I refuse to put them through what I've been through. I'm done."

Alma's heart was beating wildly now, causing the monitor to beep faster.

"Leta?" she said. Her voice sounded

small, even in her ears.

"I signed the paperwork. You're going to a psychiatric hospital after a bed becomes available. But this is it—"

"Leta, no—"

"You won't hear from me again," her sister stated. Once again, she squared her shoulders and resumed that arrogant stance of hers. "As far as I'm concerned, you're dead to me. That is what you wanted after all, right?"

Alma wanted to yell, no! To tell Leta that despite her actions, she didn't want to die. She only wanted the pain and confusion to stop. She wanted to be normal, just like her. To not live in terror of her moods changing, or something triggering her mania or her depression. To not live as a slave to her behavior. To be someone her sister could be proud of…

But no words came out of her mouth. Instead she simply watched as Leta turned and walked out of the room without a backwards glance.

Alma felt as if her heart was about to explode. She raised her hand from her breast to her face, covering the right side. Her left hand, she could only raise as far as her breast. She let it rest there as the tears flowed and collected in her palm. Leta had been the one constant in her life. Their relationship was strained, but they were sisters, they were family. How could she leave now? How could she walk away?

It's your fault. All your fault.

The guilt started again, reminding her of her failures.

You should have dug deeper into your wrists, then you would have bled out faster.

And drowned Noah in your blood.

More guilt. She thought about him…about Noah…

That poor boy…

She didn't mean for him to get involved. She had walked away.

The first time, but then you dragged him back in and left him there.

I just wanted to see what it would be like to be with someone like him. I just wanted to be normal for a little while.

You're not normal. Look at you. What normal person slices open their wrists?

Stop.

You didn't deserve him.

Stop!

You are nothing compared to him. Nothing.

A nurse rushed into the room as Alma's heart monitor beeped violently.

Twenty-Two

NOAH DROVE ONTO THE GRAVEL parking lot of Mister Bill's Bookstore and pulled into his usual spot. Except it wasn't his anymore; he had been fired the previous day for failing to show up to work, all because he dared to take initiative in regards to the opposite sex, only to have it ruin his life and leave him jobless, with memories he didn't want.

And I thought Sage was bad, he considered as he turned the engine off. Noah let out a loud snort then exited the car. He had hitched a ride home from the hospital with a couple of paramedics who were gracious enough to ask him about everything else except his emergency room visit. Vera was a lovely woman (and the pie was delicious) but talking about what happened was not something he wanted to do. How was he supposed to live down the fact that this girl had tried to take her life while lying in his arms? Hell, if he was supposed to be the spokesman for mankind, was this the experience they were missing? While women dreamed of happily-ever-after's, men were stuck with a reality that included women who were certifiable? Who planned their endings from the start and focused solely on themselves as they bled over their bed partners?

Noah though about Alma lying in his arms, close to death, her wrists open, her countenance death-like… Did she not give him any consideration as she did what she did? Did she not think about how he would feel in the morning? God, what if he had slept through the night? He would have been visiting a funeral home instead of a hospital.

And the sister! *Oh my God*, he thought. The whole family was crazy. She was controlling and judgmental; and for a moment, Noah felt sorry for Alma if she had to deal with that woman on a regular basis.

His hands clenched up and Noah realized he was angry again. Every time he thought about Alma, he became irritated. And bitter. And regretful. He had spent the evening in his apartment, thinking about Alma and after a sleepless night, he decided he was done. He refused to give her any pity. Let her have her screwed-up life, just as long as she stayed out of his. He had a life to put back together, a job to beg for. And he couldn't do that focused on what happened. He should have let her walk out of his life the first time around, but it was too late to change that. He learned his lesson. He was fine without the drama that came with the fairer sex.

Noah willed himself to calm down. He took several deep breaths and proceeded towards the bookstore. Quick strides brought him to the front door faster than he was ready. With another deep breath, he stepped inside, where he found Cass and Jada behind the front counter, doing what they normally did this early in the morning—nothing. Well, Jada was doing her nails, and Cass was watching her, but all-in-all, their actions amounted to nothing...until they saw him. Then Cass perked up. She was getting ready to speak, when Noah rushed past the front counter and into the store. He needed to talk to Bill, not her.

Noah made his way through the aisles to the back, where the office was located. As he reached his destination though, he slowed his steps. Yes, he was ready to beg, but that didn't mean he wanted to. In fact, he was having second thoughts. Would it be so hard to find another job? One that didn't include working with the public? Or young, nosy coworkers?

"Noah!"

Bill's sharp tone drew him out his thoughts. There was no backing out now. He straightened up and walked into the office. His boss, or rather, former boss, was seated behind his desk, the surface covered with papers and books. There was a computer in there, but it had been a long while since he had seen it last.

"Come to beg for your job back?"

Noah cleared his throat.

"Yes, sir."

The older man looked him up and down, glaring at him disapprovingly. Noah turned away when it became uncomfortable. When he dared to glance back at Bill, the man was still staring at him, as though trying to decide if he should rehire him or throw him out.

"Sit down," Bill eventually said.

Noah promptly obeyed.

"I inherited this store from my brother, you know that. Can't sell the damn thing, though it would make me the happiest man in the world if I could. Love books, hate the business, you know all this. You've been a good employee; you make my job easy. So, explain to me what happened. You leave the store in the care of those two dimwits up front, then you don't show up to work the next day. Help me understand."

Noah started to answer, but Bill continued. Apparently, the question was rhetorical.

"When I met you, you were a scrawny kid out of high school. You're still scrawny, but you're responsible and level-headed. I hired them as a favor, but you, I took a chance on you. Was I wrong?"

Bill paused, giving Noah a chance to explain himself. Noah, for his part, had his answer ready, having rehearsed it all morning. He cleared his throat and said, "I had a lapse of judgment...I swear it won't happen again.

Now that the words had been spoken out loud, Noah decided they didn't impart the regret he felt. In fact, he sounded like he was eighteen-years-old again and begging for a job.

Bill sighed.

"As a manager, I need you to show better judgment, girl or no girl. Do you understand what I'm saying?"

"Yes."

"Then, let's not have this conversation again. Understood?"

"Yes."

"Get to work," he grumbled and returned his attention to the paperwork in front of him.

Noah arose, surprised at the ease with which he had gained employment once more. The truth was, though, it wasn't easy. He had lost focus and had to swallow his pride. He let some woman distract him from his priorities, but no more. He would concentrate on what was truly important.

"Thank you," he stated, hoping Bill could hear the sincerity in his voice.

The man didn't look up, only waved him out.

Noah turned to go, ready to go find his apron and begin dealing with the inventory in the stockroom that he was sure the girls hadn't touch in his absence, when Bill called him back.

"Was she worth it?" the man asked him.

Noah didn't want to talk about it, but he couldn't not respond to the man who had given him his job back.

"No," he replied and left the office, before any other question came up. He rushed to the stockroom, which was adjacent to the office and found the corner where his desk was located. It was more of a catch-all with four legs, but it had been designated and he willingly accepted it. Noah pulled out the stool and sat down. He let out the breath he had been holding, then took in another one. He had thought talking to Bill would be the hard part of his day, but now that it was done and over with, he decided facing Cass was going to prove more difficult. He knew Jada wouldn't care as much, but Cass would want every minute detail.

Well, she wasn't getting any.

Noah got started on the inventory, letting

the work sidetrack him from his thoughts. It wasn't until lunch time that he ventured into the store to stock books. There were a couple of customers in the store, browsing. He passed by them without a word and walked over to the paranormal romance section. The day's new arrival pitted changelings against humans in the quest to bed the perfect woman, who couldn't choose between the two. While the notion of love and romance already nauseated Noah, he found the story itself so ridiculous, he couldn't imagine wasting time reading it. He was so busy moving books around on the shelf and critiquing them in his mind that he didn't notice Cass come up behind him. She jumped up beside him and startled him.

"Geez, don't do that," he said, shaking his head.

"You've been avoiding me," she stated matter-of-factly.

"I've been working." He returned his attention to the shelves.

"No, you've been avoiding me. Just own it."

"Fine," he muttered, trying to move as quickly as possible so as to get back to the storeroom. Sure, she and Jada could wander back there, but they didn't, often because he or Bill would put them to work—real work. "Whatever you say."

"So, what happened? You skipped out and then didn't show up yesterday."

Noah sighed, his nerves on edge. He didn't want to do this.

"Nothing."

"Something happened."

"Nothing happened."

"Come on, Noah. Give me something. It was so romantic how everything occurred."

He stopped working.

"Leave it alone, Cass," he warned, agitation in his voice.

"Hey, I'm not asking you to kiss-and-tell, just tell me her name and maybe—"

"For Christ's sake, stop!" he yelled. "Just stop already!"

Cass shrunk back away from him, stunned.

Noah immediately regretted his outburst and apologized, "Look, I…I'm sorry. I—"

"No, I get it," she acknowledged. Still, she sounded hurt. "You just want to be left alone so I'll leave you alone."

She pushed past him and walked out of the aisle. Noah sighed. He didn't mean to raise his voice at her—he wasn't the type to easily anger. And he couldn't blame Cass, she was being her usual self. It was Alma; he hadn't been his normal self since meeting Alma. It frustrated him to know that in such a minimal amount of time, she had changed his world. And having made her exit so grandiose, he was stuck with the repercussions of her actions.

Dammit!

Noah ran his hands over face and exhaled. What was he supposed to do now?

Get back to work. What else is there to do?

He finished up with the shelf and returned to the stockroom. He skipped lunch and spent the rest of the afternoon catching up on his work. He didn't have to worry about avoiding Cass, or Jada, because they were avoiding him now. Or Cass was…Jada gazed at him menacingly. She and Cass didn't often see eye-to-eye, but apparently now they had a common enemy, making the atmosphere between them tense.

The end of the day came, and the girls left without any fanfare. Noah followed shortly, leaving Bill to close the store. He picked up some dinner and headed home. His footfall was slow as he walked into his apartment. It was a small one-bedroom flat he had lived in for several years now; and while his furniture was scarce, it was home.

Except tonight it seemed…empty.

Noah brushed aside his thoughts, grabbed a cold soda from the fridge and plopped down on the couch. He turned the television on and found a program to watch—background noise. He unwrapped his burger and bit into it. Salty. Hearty. Decent.

Bite after bite, Noah filled his belly as he watched the show, not really hungry, not really paying attention. After a while, he stopped eating, leaving half a burger and a handful of fries, and mindlessly watched as one program turned into another. Eventually, Noah fell asleep on the couch.

He woke up a couple of hours later, when his bladder began calling for his attention. He made his way to the bathroom, where he relieved himself, then returned to the couch. He sprawled himself across the cushions and channel-surfed, looking for something worth watching. But nothing was. Disillusioned, he turned the television off and looked around the space he called home. It was dark, but he knew where everything was, every little nook and cranny, every object he owned. He had been so proud when he moved in and was able to finally purchase furniture and the big-screen television he had been eying for a while. Granted, some of it was second-hand, but it was his. And what did it amount to? Nothing. He had no close family, no real friends—this much was not news to him. What surprised him though was that he wasn't as content as he had always claimed to be. He was lonely and miserable; and worse than that, he was now aware of it.

Twenty-Three

NOAH LOOKED AT HIS WATCH: it was almost closing time and he was getting antsy about leaving the store. Bill had left an hour earlier, and Cass and Jada were chatting away, oblivious of their surroundings, oblivious of him. It had been a couple of days since Noah's outburst and there had been few words spoken between them. He wanted to apologize, but it seemed pointless.

Everything seemed pointless now.

Noah looked at his watch again. There was nowhere he needed to be, he just didn't want to be there anymore. He straightened up a few shelves, eying the last two customers with impatience. They were regulars and knew what time the store closed. However, they too ignored him.

I might as well be invisible.

Noah sighed and walked up front to where Cass and Jada were holding down the counter.

"You guys can go home," he said, using the most neutral tone he could muster. It didn't work though: the girls looked him up and down and made condescending sounds as they gathered their things and walked past him. The door chime sounded as they exited the store.

"You're welcome," he muttered, then stationed himself behind the counter to await the final customers. He thought about what he could do once he left. Perhaps he could go to a movie or hang out…somewhere. Where did people his age socialize?

The bell sounded again. Noah looked up in time to see a young woman with pink hair jump in front of him.

"Noah!" she exclaimed. It was Hedy, his landlord's daughter. She was a short, petite woman, whose hair had been green last time he saw her. He couldn't remember if she was still a teenager or legal in the eyes of the law. His first thought was younger, given her behavior, but he could be wrong. Women were not his expertise.

"Hey," he stated, surprised. She had been in a couple of times for art books, but nothing more. "What are you doing here?"

"Daddy dropped me off downtown to go shopping. Thought I'd stop in and say hello, how are you, my roof furniture is ruined, you haven't said anything about it, anything new?"

Noah took in a deep breath, embarrassed. Since that 'night', he had avoided going up to the roof or following up with the landlord to inquire on the damages. He wasn't dodging his responsibility, he just didn't want to discuss the events of that evening, or the person responsible for it. Noah was determined to put both out of his mind for good, which was something he was sure Hedy wasn't going to let him do. She had been by his place a couple of times, but he had pretended to not be home. It worked—until now. He should have been man enough to at least apologize, but it seemed he wasn't man at all.

"Listen, I—"

"Don't sweat it," she interrupted, leaning forward on the counter. "I wanted to redecorate anyway."

She smiled sweetly, resting her elbows in front of her and her head in her hands. There was a twinkle in her eye. Noah had to wonder if there was any truth to what Al… to what was said about Hedy being sweet on him. Had he missed it in all the time he had known her? Not that it would have made a difference since she was much too young for him and he was in no way attracted to her. She was like a cousin to him.

"So how much longer are you here for?" she asked.

"As soon as they leave," Noah said quietly nodding over towards the remaining customers.

"Tell them to go," Hedy suggested.

"They're customers."

"It's closing time."

"They have money, they can stay. I'll wait, I don't mind," he lied.

"That's crazy. Just tell them to go. Here I'll do it for you." And before Noah could stop her, she bounced off the counter and approached the two. She spoke to them in a hushed tone and though Noah couldn't hear her, he could see how effective her words were: the two immediately abandoned the books they were looking at and headed to the door without looking at him. Noah thought to ask Hedy what she said, but then realized he didn't want to know. He left the counter and locked the door as Hedy strolled back up to the front of the store, an arrogant smirk on her face.

"Aren't you going to ask me?"

He shook his head.

"Nope. Like you said, it's closing time."

"Great. So, can I get a ride?"

Noah figured this was probably her objective from the start, but he didn't care.

"Yeah, sure, come on."

He turned off lights then exited through the back door. Hedy followed, skipping.

Yeah, she's definitely younger.

They walked around to the front of the

store, where his car was parked. Noah opened the door for her; however, she just seemed amused by the gesture. He shook his head and got in the car. Once he was out of the parking lot and moving in the direction of their apartment building, Hedy said, "Let's get some coffee."

Noah thought briefly about arguing against it, knowing she was likely going to bring up the roof incident again, but he had nothing waiting for him at home. Maybe he could weather the questions if it meant he didn't have to spend time with himself or with his thoughts. Without answering, he made a U-turn and headed towards the coffee house down the street from the bookstore. He found a parking spot and helped his neighbor out of the car. She smiled and placed her arm through his, making him wonder if he was enabling a crush.

You've got a big head now, huh?

They ordered their coffee and found a seat at one of the more remote tables. Hedy gazed at him, still smiling. Noah looked around.

"So, you've been avoiding me," she finally said.

He sighed. Apparently, this was the impression he was giving lately.

"Not you specifically," he replied. "Just everyone in general."

"Do you want to talk about it?" Hedy asked, picking up her spoon.

Ugh. Why did everyone want to talk?

"Please don't take this the wrong way, but I really don't."

"Fair enough," she stated, and paused to stir her coffee. When she finished, she placed her spoon on the table and said, "I take it others have taken it the wrong way."

Noah bit the inside of his lip. He shouldn't have said anything.

"I went off on one my coworkers. She's still mad at me."

She sat back, feigned astonishment on her face. "You? Go off?"

He rolled his eyes.

Hedy laughed, then asked, "So who was she?"

"Cass. The older one."

"No, I mean the girl on the roof."

And the inquiry starts…

"No one," Noah muttered.

"Well, *no one* bled all over the furniture and Daddy is on me about letting others upstairs."

"I'm sorry. I'll pay for it."

"That's not why I'm here, Noah. Just tell me who she was. Or is. Hopefully."

Noah grunted. Actually grunted. Like a caveman. He didn't want to talk, but if anyone deserved an explanation of events, it was Hedy. Plus, if he was truly honest with himself, this whole affair was eating him from the inside out. No, he didn't want to talk, he *needed* to in order to get everything off his chest—the anger at being used, the shock, the hurt, the betrayal…

God, now his life sounded like a soap opera.

Betrayed by the one he cared for. Left to deal with the aftermath of an…accident. Lashing out at the ones closest to him…

He guffawed, then realized he had done it out loud. He looked at Hedy, who appeared amused.

"Alma. That's her name," he said.

"Pretty name," Hedy commented.

He nodded his head in agreement. And because he had opened the door for discussion, he continued, telling his neighbor about the day and night he spent with Alma.

"So, what would have happened in the morning, had she not attempted suicide?" Hedy asked. The word rolled off her tongue so easily.

"I don't know. It probably would've been awkward. She kept insisting she didn't want to see me. Now I know why," he replied with resignation.

"But if it was up to you, what would have

happened?" she repeated.

Noah felt relieved after sharing as much as he did, and he appreciated Hedy's insistence that he do so. However, this was one question he didn't want to answer because he still wanted the same thing, he still wanted to see Alma and to get to know her. But if he said it, if he acknowledged his desire, knowing what he knew now, then he was a bigger fool for saying it.

When he failed to respond, Hedy spoke up. But her chipper tone had changed: she was serious now.

"Do you remember about two years ago when I was 'visiting' with my grandmother?" she began. Noah nodded. "I was depressed. I wanted to die. I wanted the pain to end. Depression just isn't in your head alone, you know. It affects your body. It makes you ache, physically. It makes you hurt. It changes who you are. It changed who I was. And I decided I'd had enough and wanted to die. So, I swallowed half a bottle of aspirin. But the pills weren't enough, and in my stupor, I called my brother and told him what I did. They got me to the ER, where my stomach was pumped. Then I was admitted to a psychiatric hospital for several months where I underwent treatment for depression.

"While the whole experience was

horrible, the worst part were the paramedics, who felt I was simply wasting their time. I was in and out of consciousness, but I heard them talking, like I wasn't even there. 'I just wanted attention.' Or 'I was a spoiled brat who was using the time and resources that could go to people who really needed help." Or 'if I was really serious, I would have taken more pills.' But you know what? I felt so hopeless, all I could think about was ending it all. I didn't think about how many pills I needed to take, or what kind of effect they would have on me. I just wanted to be done. I didn't want to fight or hide behind smiles anymore. I didn't want to pretend that I was okay."

Hedy paused, looking down at her drink. She suddenly appeared older than what she was. Noah recalled her absence and realized he hadn't once inquired about her. He was friendly with her family. He spoke with her father often enough about things not related to the building—the weather, whatever game was on, traffic... Shouldn't he have asked about Hedy instead of making small talk?

"I am better now. I'm on medication and I understand why I need to be, but maybe Alma does not. Or maybe she doesn't have a reason to be. I'm not trying to tell you what to do, you may not even like the girl, but maybe you can try to see this experience through her eyes, because it wasn't nothing. It wasn't her just crying for attention or wasting someone else's time. She was calling out for help."

The words hit him hard. Noah didn't know what to say, but he was sure Hedy didn't expect him to say anything. Apparently, this had become her mission in life, and he respected her for that. But at the same time, he despised the fact that he was the one being charged with saving Alma.

Hedy continued talking. Noah stirred his coffee, pretending to listen, but in the back of his mind, he thought about Alma. He thought about how she looked and felt, not when he first met her, but when he last saw her, when he last touched her. His heart hurt seeing her so cold and lifeless; and it fueled the contempt he felt for her, knowing she had plotted to end her life in his arms.

But Hedy was right, he didn't know. He had no clue what she was going through. And more than that, he didn't know who she really was. There was too much about this whole situation he didn't comprehend, too much about Alma he didn't understand, especially her disease. She had disregarded his feelings but perhaps Alma wasn't playing with him as much as she was succumbing to a bad situation. He needed to find out. He needed to know more.

"Your coffee is getting cold," Hedy said, breaking him out of his thoughts. He glanced down at his cup and realized he hadn't drunk any of it. Neither did he want to. His appetite was lost. He was anxious again, but for a different reason: he needed to get back to the bookstore.

"I guess I'm done with it," he said.

Hedy shrugged her shoulders and started cleaning up her side of the table, moving her napkin and used sugar packets into her empty cup.

"Good timing then, because I have to get going." She smirked then added, "I told Daddy you'd have me home about half an hour ago. I'm sure he's pissed that I'm late."

Making a mental note to avoid his landlord for the next week or so, Noah escorted Hedy out to his car and took her home as quickly—and as legally—as possible. She thanked him, kissed him on the cheek and ran inside the building, turning back briefly to wave at him before disappearing inside.

Noah returned to the bookstore. He entered the way he left, through the back door and into the storeroom. He didn't turn on the lights because he knew exactly where he was going—the health section. Bill didn't carry as many medical books as he did romances, but he had enough to cover the basics and that's all Noah needed right now, a basic understanding of what Alma was dealing with. And having arrived at the correct section, Noah perused the shelves until he found the right book.

Twenty-Four

NOAH HAD A PLAN… OKAY, IT was more of an idea, but it still counted. Unfortunately, he needed help from Cass, which was something he probably wasn't going to get, since she was still mad at him. She wasn't even talking to him anymore. He had greeted her that morning hoping to talk to her, but she only frowned at him, as if he was a mangled piece of roadkill in her path. Noah considered abandoning his plan, but when he thought about all that was at stake, he knew he couldn't give up.

While Jada was distracted by Pete, who seemed to be a constant fixture in the store lately, Noah conjured up a healthy dose of courage and approached Cass. She was supposed to be going through the catalog, looking for a specific book for a customer, but instead she was reading one of the paperbacks slated for donation. He cleared his throat to get her attention, but she didn't stop reading, nor did she acknowledge him. She was ignoring him.

With a sigh, Noah cleared his throat once more and said, "Her name is Alma."

Cass blinked a couple of times, then

pursed her lips, trying her best not to look up at him. She resisted as long as she could before curiosity got the best of her. She looked up, her eyebrow raised, and her head cocked as she sized him up. She was guarded, but open, which was all Noah needed. He was still hesitant to talk about the whole situation, but he did so anyway, recounting the events of the date and culminating in the trip to the hospital.

"I was upset, and I didn't want to talk about her because…of the way things ended, but—"

"Oh my God," Cass lamented, her face a myriad of expressions. "I am so sorry." Without warning, she reached over and pulled him in for a hug.

Noah hadn't figured on this response and was a little embarrassed by it.

"Cass…"

She let him go; and with a teary expression, said, "If I had known, I wouldn't have pushed you to go after her—"

"No, Cass, listen—"

"God, I would have been mad at me too…I am so sorry, Noah…"

Noah thought to just bite his tongue and let her finish, like he always did, but not today.

"It's okay!" he exclaimed, taking her by

the shoulders. The action and tone stunned her, and she stared at him in surprise. He let go and composed himself, before he lost nerve, or momentum. "I want to go see her, but I need your help."

She studied him briefly then asked, "Are you sure? I mean, she's..."

She made meaningless gestures with her hands, trying to avoid the one that meant something: her finger pointing towards her temple, dancing in a circle, the universal sign for crazy. Noah had no doubt that Alma might take that moniker as her own, but from his understanding, she was simply...

"Sick?" he offered. Not that he was an expert now, he had read only one book. But something in him was already protective over Alma.

Cass dropped her arm and nodded.

"Alright, sick then. Have you thought this through?"

Since his chat with Hedy, it was all Noah thought about. Yes, in the time he spent with Alma, there were enough red flags to drive most people away, but he didn't see that. He saw...Alma. Looks, yes, God, yes. She was hot. But beyond that, he saw her smile and felt the warmness that emanated from her soul. He looked into her eyes and saw a meekness that defied her vulnerability. He watched her movements and saw meticulous, thoughtful action. He couldn't explain it, even to himself, but when Noah saw Alma, he saw life itself.

Ugh, you sound like you've been spending too much time in the romance section.

"Yes," he finally told Cass.

She smiled broadly.

"Then I'm happy to help. What do you need from me?"

"Can you cover for me while I go out to the hospital?"

Bill was gone for the day, and while he trusted Noah with the store, he didn't trust the girls. So, Noah was risking his job again by asking. But he had decided to visit Alma at the spur of the moment; and he couldn't wait until the evening, after he closed the store: visiting hours would be over. He had to take a chance.

Cass' enthusiasm faded.

"You're coming back, right?"

Noah smiled sheepishly at her.

"Yes, I'm coming back."

"Okay," she said. "I'll cover."

"Thank you," he replied and turned to leave. Then he remembered Jada. She would never let him live down the fact that Alma was his first date since Sage and the end result was her trying to commit suicide. While technically this was the truth, it was the also the last thing his male ego wanted to be branded with. He returned to the sales counter and added, "Please don't tell Jada."

She shook her head understandingly.

"Go, I got this," she told him, then added, "Get her flowers. She'll like that."

Noah wasn't sure Alma would, but he nodded and rushed off. He drove straight to the hospital and parked in a visitor's spot, excited but also nervous. She had been adamant about not seeing him after their evening together, but that was also before her 'attempt'. Would she be upset that she lived? Like Hedy said, perhaps she felt she had no reason to be alive. So maybe he could be that reason.

Noah peered at himself in the rearview mirror. He ran a hand over his thin face, several days' growth on it and wondered what it was exactly that someone like Alma saw in him. Was he reason enough to live? Or did she only kiss him, like she said, because she needed something to do? Why did she kiss him?

Knowing if he sat in the car long enough, he would talk himself out of seeing Alma, Noah exited the vehicle and marched into the hospital. He was ready to approach the information desk, when he noticed the gift shop on his right. Maybe flowers were a good idea.

After purchasing a colorful bouquet of carnations, Noah walked up to the information desk and the two nurses sitting behind it. In all his excitement, he didn't consider the one thing he would need to see Alma: her last name. He still didn't know it. He had no information about her except her first name and her 'ailment'. Unfortunately, this wasn't enough.

"I'm sorry, sir," one of the nurses told him. "We can't help you."

"I came in with her a few days ago. She had…she was…" He felt more comfortable with the word 'suicide'; however, he didn't want to go around telling everyone she had attempted it. "Maybe I can check with emergency or intensive care? I think that's where the doctor said she would be."

"We can't allow you to just walk around, disturbing staff and patients."

"I just want to see her."

"Are you family?"

"No."

"Who are you to her?"

"A…friend."

The nurse shook her head.

"I'm sorry, sir. If she is in intensive care, then only family members are permitted to visit."

A security guard joined them at the desk. He didn't say anything, just glowered at Noah.

"Can you at least tell me how she is?" Noah pleaded.

"We cannot give out information on patients," she said with finality in her tone. "I think it's in your best interest to go."

Noah could see he wasn't going to get anywhere, and while the thought of sneaking past them did occur to him, he knew he would likely fail. He walked back outside certain he would never get to see Alma again.

Noah dropped onto the bench beside the entrance and brooded. He couldn't walk away. He needed to do something. He needed an actual plan this time, maybe an accomplice, someone to distract the security guard and the nurses, while he wandered around.

No, that was stupid. He didn't have all afternoon to walk around. He promised Cass he'd be back.

Maybe if he had someone do it for him. Someone on the inside.

Inspiration struck: Vera, the nurse in the Heart Center who bought him pie and coffee. She said she was available if he needed help and this constituted as needing help...right?

There was only one way to find out.

Noah checked his watch. He didn't know her schedule, but if she was working, he could catch her at the same entrance he met her at before. He circumnavigated the exterior of the campus, arriving at the emergency entrance minutes later. Noah took a seat on the bench where he sat last time and waited. He passed the time by watching emergency crews go in and out with patients. This was definitely a profession he would not excel in. The slower the pace (and less urgent the matter), the better. He couldn't even imagine being responsible for someone else's life like that.

"So those lovely flowers are to thank me for the time and compassion I showed you, correct?" Noah heard after a while. He looked up and saw a heavy-set woman with a kind expression on her face approaching him. It was Vera.

"Ah…," he replied. Or rather sounded out. He should have gotten her something in exchange for the favor he was getting ready to ask her for.

She removed her bags from her shoulder and sat beside him.

"How are you doing? You're not covered in blood, so hopefully better."

Noah smiled sheepishly.

"Better, yes. Thank you for the advice.

You were right."

Vera sat up a little straighter and smiled.

"Music to a woman's ears."

He chuckled.

"So, are you here visiting your friend? How is she?"

"Well…," Noah began; and since she had opened the door to the discussion, he unloaded everything. He told her about Alma, then finished with, "I know you don't know me, but I was hoping you would at least be able to help me find out how she is."

Vera gazed at him, her light blue eyes sparkling with hope.

"I can do that."

While she ran upstairs to drop her bags off and research Alma's condition, Noah waited for her in the cafeteria. He purchased two pies and two coffees; and waited patiently. Or at least as patiently as he could. He kept looking over his shoulder to see if Vera had returned. Minutes passed and Noah grew more anxious. He had been gone from the bookstore for over an hour. Cass would think he had ditched her again.

Noah took a sip of his coffee. It was cold. He refilled both cups and sat back down to continue waiting. It seemed he was always waiting. He hated waiting.

Finally, Vera returned. She saw the pie

and coffee and smiled.

"You're sweet, aren't you?"

She took a seat across from him. Noah thought she would delay and make small talk or dig into the treat, but she didn't. Appreciatively, she updated him immediately.

"Your friend is out of intensive care."

Vera didn't sound as hopeful as her words intended.

"But...?" Noah prompted.

"She was moved to the psych ward so they could keep an eye on her. She'll be going to a psychiatric hospital beginning of next week."

While part of Noah worried whether he would be able to see her once she was transferred, he knew this was what was best for her.

"Will she get better there?" he asked.

Vera shrugged.

"It's up to her. If she feels she has a reason to live, then she'll respond to treatment and get better. But if she doesn't, then chances are she won't..."

Noah finished her thought when her voice lagged again: "And next time, she'll succeed in killing herself."

Vera nodded her head.

Both fell silent. He began his day with

such hope, but now he was slowly spiraling into despair. He couldn't be sure that Alma saw the value of her life, and the thought of not seeing her again had his heart breaking. There had to be something he could do to help her, to make her see her life was worth living.

"Noah, I've been doing this long enough to know you can't save her. She has to make that decision," Vera stated, as if reading his thoughts. "All you can do is support and encourage her; and let her know that you're there."

"How do I do that when I'm here and she's there?" he asked, waving his arm towards the main hospital building where he could only assume Alma was located.

"Do you want to see her?" Vera asked, though hesitantly. "I might get in trouble, but I should be able to get you in there."

Noah wanted to say yes, he really did, but he wondered how Alma would react to seeing him. The circumstances between them had changed dramatically. She obviously had a plan for her future that didn't include him, or rather, didn't include *a future* period. Would she be mad at him for saving her? Would she be embarrassed? Would she respond either way? Perhaps she would blame him for being stuck in her current situation. He was unapologetic about his actions, she needed help. He didn't think she would accept that. She was a free bird, a live wire. She wanted things on her terms and in her time. Her list was a prime example.

Noah reached into his back pocket and pulled out his wallet. Inside, he found Alma's list. He had stuck it in his pants the day of the suicide attempt and found it later when he changed his clothes. He threw it out, but after talking to Hedy, he retrieved it from the waste bin. There was mustard on it, in addition to blood, but it was still legible. He reread the list, every entry, every word. What she had accomplished and what she didn't. Were there things that didn't make the list that she still wanted to do? Would she consider sticking around for those?

And what about him? He had topped this list; would she ponder making a new one that included more than kissing? He would wait for her, visit her, bring her flowers and s'mores. He wasn't boyfriend material, but he would try. He would change—hell, he had already changed. He was doing things that were outside his normal behavior. He had found the courage to talk to people he would have never approached before. He pursued what he wanted instead of giving up easily. He was learning and developing empathy.

Noah was a better man after spending only twenty-four hours with Alma; what kind of man would he be after weeks, or months, or even years with her?

But this is a death list. Alma wanted to die. Everything she did points to that.

Except the kiss. She was saying goodbye to everyone, except him. He was a stranger, which made the kiss a 'hello' of sorts, a sliver of light in a dark corner…right?

You're reading into things.

Maybe he was, but there was only one way to find out.

Alma made it clear she doesn't want to discuss the kiss.

But that was before. Things have changed.

Except Noah didn't believe that for one second. Alma was head-strong; and the sterile environment of the hospital didn't lend itself to personal conversations. He had only been hospitalized once, and though the occasion wasn't the worst he'd experienced, he was only too happy to go home. Perhaps Alma was the same. If they were somewhere else, out in the world, watching a sunset or enjoying the city lights, maybe she would talk to him.

But she needs to be in the hospital.

But what if she could leave for a little bit, before she was moved to the psychiatric hospital? One last hurrah…

That will require help.

Noah looked away from the list and up at Vera. Where he lacked patience, she abounded in it, waiting quietly for him to answer her question. Yes, he wanted to see Alma. He wanted to help her, to give her a reason to live and get better, to let her know she had people waiting for her, who cared for her, but he couldn't do that here in the hospital. He had to get her out, just for a few hours.

And as he gazed at Vera, Noah knew what he had to do. First though, he would have to call Cass and let her know he would not be coming back to work.

Twenty-Five

HUMMING A TUNE SHE HEARD earlier that day, Vera slowly pushed Alma's wheelchair through the halls. She didn't have permission to do so, but after a stirring conversation with Noah, she agreed to help him with his 'plan'. However, she had one condition.

"She has to want to go," Vera told him as he gulped down his coffee. He nodded in agreement, but she wasn't sure he fully understood the situation. "Noah, did you hear me?" He set his cup down and gave her his attention. "I like to think I'm a pretty good judge of character, and to be honest, you don't worry me. But you have to understand, you can't save her. She's going to have to make that decision herself."

"I get what you're saying," he assured her.

"So, if she sees you and wants to turn around, you have to accept she's not ready. If you visit her later at the hospital and she doesn't want anything to do with you, you have to assent to what she wants. And if she doesn't respond to treatment and takes her life, it's not your fault. Do you understand?"

His excitement waned a bit, but not his

confidence.

"Yeah," he said simply. "I get it."

Vera sighed. She was a hypocrite. Didn't she drag a blood-covered young man into the cafeteria to partake of pie and coffee, just to get him to talk?

She changed the subject.

"Just be sure to have her back before my shift ends."

"I will," he said.

"Good. Now I need your license."

He frowned.

"For what?

"You didn't think I was going to let you just walk out with me not knowing anything about you, did you? I'm going to make a copy of it, just in case I'm wrong and you turn out to be some kind of serial killer or something. I don't think I am, but if there's even a fraction of a possibility that you're anything but a sincere, young man with a serious crush on a lovely Latina, at least then I'll have all your information to give to the police. You should be warned though: I heard the sister is a real ball-buster."

Of course, the sister was hardly a concern at this juncture. Instead, Vera was worried for Alma. Wearing a pair of hospital scrub pants and a t-shirt Vera found in a closet, the woman wasn't very responsive. She simply sat in the wheelchair, her head turned to the side, her wrists bandaged up. Her hair was pulled back in a ponytail and her complexion was pale. She didn't argue with Vera when she got her, simply did as she was directed. No words, no sounds, no emotions. She was oblivious to everything around her, a fraction of the woman Vera imagined she once was.

The portly nurse turned the corner towards the clinic exit where Noah was waiting for them with his car. She continued humming, a little louder now so that Alma could hear her. She kept her steady pace until she reached the doors. They slid open, patients and medical staff alike walking in and out. It was a busy intersection, which was what Vera wanted when she chose the location to meet Noah. No one would see them amidst the crowd. And with the psych ward being understaffed, their success was all but guaranteed. No one would miss Alma. Her part of the plan was complete.

Vera pushed the wheelchair through the doors and stopped outside, where Noah was parked. He stood beside his car in the patient loading zone, awkwardly holding the bouquet of flowers he had with him earlier. Vera moved around to the front of the wheelchair and crouched in front of Alma, balancing herself on her tip-toes.

"Do you know him, sweetheart?" she asked.

Alma looked up at Noah and seemed to recognize him. At least that's what Vera thought. The poor girl had such a lost expression on her face, she couldn't be sure. Alma eventually turned back to Vera and nodded.

"Well, I want you to know this is unconventional, but I think it might help you. He came to me earlier and asked to see you and take you out for a few hours to help you. I told him yes, that I would help him, but you don't have to go if you don't want to," Vera stated.

Alma turned her head to the side and stared at the concrete.

"It would just be for the afternoon. You'll be back by evening. And it might do you some good to get some fresh air. But if you're uncomfortable leaving with him, then tell me and I'll take you back to your room. You don't have to go."

Still, Alma didn't say anything.

Vera's instincts kicked in and she found herself wanting to save Alma herself. A hypocrite for certain, but with a good heart. She cupped her face in her hands and drew her gaze to her.

"Listen, whatever you decide, I want you

to know that you are loved, and your life does matter."

Tears formed in Alma's eyes as she gazed at Vera. There seemed to be a battle brewing within her, Alma wanting to believe Vera, but struggling to do so. Vera thought to keep talking, but the girl deserved real hope, not empty words. She'd said everything she needed to say; the rest was up to Alma.

"Okay," she finally said, a single tear sliding down her cheek. Vera wiped it off, kissed her forehead and stood upright. She pushed the wheelchair to the car and Noah. Having patiently waited this entire time, he rushed to meet them and open the door to his vehicle. He seemed nervous, offering Alma the flowers, but holding onto them in case she was weak or uninterested. Alma for her part, focused only on standing and getting into the car. She sank into her chair and let Noah buckle her in. Once he was finished, he shut the door and turned to Vera.

"Before my shift ends," she warned him.

"I will," he promised, then kissed her cheek. "Thank you."

She smiled and waved him off.

"Just be careful," she said.

He hurried around the car to the driver's side, got in and drove off. Vera watched them go. Part of her worried about what might happen. They had exchanged mobile numbers so he could call her if anything went wrong, but nothing had so far, and Vera knew the chances were nothing would. Still she hoped Noah's plan worked, for Alma's sake.

"DADDY!" ZOEY yelled as she disappeared into the house.

Leta grabbed the rest of the gift bags and her purse; and followed after her daughter. The party was a success. Each of the girls who attended went home happy and dazzling, having enjoyed a few hours of primping and pampering. Leta's mother-in-law had helped corral the girls at the salon and was able to enjoy a pedicure as her reward. Of course, Leta had to pass but she would make an appointment later in the week for herself.

She walked in through the back door and dropped everything on the kitchen counter. She could hear Zoey running around with her cousins, who were similar in age. They belonged to Owen's brother, who was only too happy to send them with his parents so that he could enjoy some quiet time with his wife.

"How did it go?" Owen asked. A beer

bottle in hand, he walked over and kissed her.

"Tiring, but great. Did Zoey show you her manicure? I heard her calling you."

"She wanted to know if they could go to the park to play."

"Did you tell her no? It'll be dark soon."

He smiled at her, amused by her concern.

"Nope. I told her she could go. She could even take the car, that way they could stay longer," he replied, tongue-in-cheek.

Leta frowned, unappreciative of his humor at the moment. He laughed and kissed her forehead.

"Relax, baby, they're upstairs. Mom and Dad are in the living room. Come join us and get off your feet."

"I will. I'm just going to put a few things away."

Owen shook his head. He didn't believe her, but he didn't argue either.

"Don't be too long then," he stated with resignation. He turned to leave, but then remembered, "You got a package today. It's there on the table."

"Who's it from?"

"I didn't look at it."

Owen disappeared into the living room, where Leta could already hear the game in play. She didn't know if it was football, basketball or baseball, but it almost didn't matter, Owen and his father would watch anything.

Left alone in the kitchen, Leta put away the extra gift bags she brought home. Once she was done, she decided to enjoy her family. But there were dishes in the sink. If she did those quickly, she wouldn't have to come back to do them later. She opted to clean up. Then wipe down the counters. Then sweep up. Twenty minutes later, the kitchen was spotless and Leta felt good about relaxing. The game was still on and she could hear the girls upstairs playing in Zoey's room. Leta started to exit the kitchen when she remembered the package. She walked over to the table and picked up the large, rectangular envelope with her name clearly written on the front. There was no return address, but she recognized the handwriting as Alma's.

Without even meaning to, Leta dropped into the chair beside her. She hadn't thought about her sister in days, purposely. She was done running through hoops for her. Owen argued with her in the beginning, but he finally assented to her point-of-view. This was what was best for everyone.

So why was her hand shaking then?

She's dead to me, and I'm dead to her, Leta told herself. It didn't matter that she didn't believe her own words—they were true. And whatever game Alma had played wasn't going to change it.

Leta composed herself and opened the package. Inside was a book, and a cloth. She unwrapped the latter and discovered a hummingbird necklace with a small note that simply read,

For Zoey.

It was Alma's necklace, the one Zoey loved so much. Alma was giving it to her, not so much as a birthday gift but a goodbye present.

The thought made Leta mad. This was the legacy her sister was going to leave her only niece? A cheap piece of jewelry? Leta thought about taking everything and dumping it in the trash, but curiosity got the best of her. What else did Alma send?

Leta picked up the book: it was a photo album with a suede cover decorated with fabric flowers and a die-cut hummingbird. On the cover was etched the words, *La Vida*. It was beautiful. Leta ran her hand over it to get a feel for the material. The hummingbird was strictly Alma's thing, but everything else was Leta. She loved the look and craftiness of it. She opened the album and found an inscription.

Leta,

I hope this is how you choose to remember me instead of all the trouble I caused you. Te amo. Alma.

Leta turned the page and immediately started crying. On the first page was a picture of a beautiful, young Latina with two small girls on her lap. The woman had her arms lovingly around the girls, who looked up adoringly at their mother. Leta recalled taking the photo. Her mom was spending the afternoon with them, after taking the day off of work. They had gone 'hiking' at a local park and stopped at convenience store to get all the junk food they wanted for dinner. Leta remembered the day, not because of what they did, but because that day, her *Mami* was the adult and she and her sister were the kids. Everything was as it was supposed to be.

Sheet after sheet, pictures of her mother filled the parchment. She was a shapely and attractive woman with a head full of straight black hair and skin that was tanned and flawless. And her smile…Leta had forgotten how her smile lit up whatever she room she was in. It was her later years she recalled whenever she thought of her mother, but looking through the photos now, Leta remembered every detail about her and Alma, who was a beautiful little girl, carefree and full of life. No different than Zoey, she thought.

How could Leta have forgotten? They were her family, her *mami* and her *hermana*. How did her view become so obscured that she stopped looking at who they were, and only saw what they became? They were her world once. She chose to be strong and suffered through a childhood no one should have to bear just so they could exist. Should she do any less now? After all, she was made strong for a reason, for *Mami* and for Alma.

Leta had to stop looking at the album, her vision blurred from all the tears. She covered her face with her hands and sobbed. She sat like this for a long time, guilt-ridden and heart-broken, lost in her thoughts. She didn't hear Owen until he was kneeling beside her.

"Honey?"

She looked at him with swollen eyes, and rather than try to explain her tears away as she might have done before, she simply threw her arms around him. Owen, for his part, didn't question the situation. He held her close to him, cooing to her as if she were a child, and she loved him more for it. Cradling her head in his arms, he promised her everything would work out and she would be alright. Leta let him comfort her, until her cries subsided, and she was able to think clearly again. Only then did she pull away from Owen, though she continued to touch him. She needed to feel him right now; she needed to know he was with her.

"I left her there."

"She's sick, Leta," he reminded her gently.

"I know. But I shouldn't have left her there like that. I shouldn't have said what I said and treated her like she was a burden."

"You were stressed."

"I was wrong. I abandoned her when she needed me the most."

Owen took a deep breath, and with no less love in his eyes, asked, "So what do you want to do?"

Leta didn't hesitate.

"I want to see her. I want to help her get better."

"Will you let *me* help *you* do that?"

She didn't pause or question his motives. Instead, she nodded, knowing that even as strong as she was, she needed someone to lean on.

"I'll ask Mom and Dad to watch the girls," he said. "You get ready and we'll go to the hospital, okay?"

Leta nodded again, but before he could slip away from her, she cupped his face in her hands and kissed him. He responded tenderly, then pulled her in one more time for a hug before releasing her to go talk to his parents.

Twenty-Six

ALMA'S BODY FELT LIKE A train ran over it, which surprised her, considering it was just her wrists she cut. She closed her eyes and turned her head towards the window, but when she did that, all she saw was the knife cutting through her skin. She felt the pain in her wrists and the pulse of her heart beating harder as the blood flowed out of her veins. Alma quickly opened her eyes, desperate to get the images out of her mind. She had not counted on surviving the suicide attempt, but now that she had, she was haunted by the memories of her actions.

"Are you okay?"

She heard the concern in Noah's voice, but she didn't respond. He was the last person she wanted to see. She didn't understand why he was there, but with a few hours out of the hospital, she didn't care either. Like before, he was convenient; and she was going to take advantage of him for a change of scenery.

"Where are we going?" she finally asked.

"Well, I thought we'd do dinner, but there're a couple of stops we need to make first."

Alma didn't react either way and simply

looked out of the window as they drove through town, the sights familiar, but inconsequential. She considered nothing, thought about nothing, felt nothing.

After a few minutes, Noah slowed the car and pulled into a parking lot. He parked in one of the first spots and turned off the engine. The area had fallen into disuse, apparent by the weeds sprouting through the concrete and the gang tags on the signs. The area was empty, save for a couple of men walking towards them.

"Here," Noah stated, handing her a long-sleeved sweater. "Put this on."

Alma turned towards him and took the garment without question. It was a little big for her, but she managed to get it on. She let her hands rest on her legs, the sleeves covering her wrists. She turned her head towards the lot once again, the men coming into the view. She didn't know the taller man, but the smaller one was familiar.

Noah lowered the window.

"Baby girl," the man called out in a raspy voice. "Baby girl."

It was Saad. He walked a little quicker until he was at her side. Then, as he had done on occasion, he reached in and patted her head.

"What are you doing here?" she asked.

"Your friend here had the folks at the mission find me. Said you weren't feeling too good," he replied. "Said you needed a friend to talk to."

Alma glanced at Noah, who was looking at the dashboard with feigned interest.

"You had us a little worried after your last visit," the man continued. "I wasn't sure what was going on, and you know the guys, they just don't get you like I do."

She tugged on her sleeves, a little embarrassed. Saad lived on the streets. She met him a year earlier when they were both hospitalized. He was unkempt and a little crazy, but he had a good heart and she often checked up on him to make sure he was doing alright.

Now he was the one checking up on her.

He continued talking, letting her know what she had missed in the days she was gone, just like they did on past visits. Alma mostly listened. She stole a glance at Noah every once in a while, who was now engrossed in the story of government conspiracies and secret experiments that Saad was telling.

"Now, I'm telling you this in confidence, because there are ears everywhere. So, I need you to promise me you won't repeat a word of what I told you."

Noah nodded.

"Absolutely."

"You can't be too careful," Saad stated, scratching his head. "I didn't believe once, but I am a full believer now. And I got the scars to show anyone who says I'm lying. You don't forget stuff like that. No, you don't."

Alma rested her hand on his shoulder. He refocused and smiled at her.

"It's always good seeing you, Angel. I gotta go, but you know I'm your friend. Just find me."

"I know, Saad," she said quietly. "Thank you."

She kissed his cheek, even though she knew it had been some time since his last shower, then she dropped her hand back onto her lap. He said his goodbyes to Noah, then rejoined his friend, who had been patiently waiting by the side of the car, smoking a cigarette. Alma felt 'less numb' than she did before.

"Did he really go through all that stuff?" Noah asked as he started the car.

She shook her head. She really didn't know.

Noah put the car in gear and was ready to drive off when Alma reached over and touched his arm. He stopped what he was doing and looked at her.

"You didn't tell him," she stated. It wasn't a question. Obviously, Noah had planned some elaborate intervention of sorts centered around her suicide attempt but if he didn't tell others why, it defeated the purpose.

"No. I figured you didn't want everybody knowing. Wade asked, but I didn't tell him either."

The man had confronted Alma a few times about his suspicions of her mental state. He offered to help but Alma turned him down each time. She didn't need help, she told him, she was fine.

God, why was she so obstinate?

"Oh, I think Glen knows though," Noah said, interrupting her thoughts.

Alma frowned.

"You talked to Glen?"

Noah nodded his head.

"He said to tell you to stop by when you're ready so he can hook you up."

Alma smiled, appreciative of their friendship.

Then it occurred to her what Noah was doing, calling everyone he had met during their day together.

"You didn't call Stan, did you? Because I'm pretty sure he doesn't want to see me."

"No, I didn't," he chuckled, then asked, "That was it. But we've got one more stop before we grab some dinner. Can you wait an hour to eat?"

Alma shrugged her shoulders and turned her gaze forward.

They arrived at their next destination in minutes. It was the animal shelter.

"Why are we here?" she asked.

"Come on, you'll see," Noah replied, as he helped her out of her seat and into the building. Inside, they were greeted by one of the volunteers, who walked them to where the kennels were located. Inside were dogs of every breed, age and color. Alma smiled. She had always wanted a dog; her mother had even promised her one, but when she died, that dream went with her. Her grandmother would not even entertain the notion of a pet. Alma understood now the woman could barely afford to feed her granddaughters, much less a dog. Still, her heart always yearned for one. And when her eyes came upon a young chocolate lab, with big eyes, she knew he was the one.

"Can I see him?" she asked the volunteer, who promptly opened his cage. The dog practically ran into her arms. He licked her face and nuzzled with her as if he too knew they were meant to be together. "What's his name?"

"Actually, he doesn't have one that we

know. Someone abandoned him and his siblings on the side of the road. An older woman found them and brought them here," the volunteer explained. "He's the only one who hasn't been adopted. Looks like he was waiting for you."

Alma smiled, trying to contain her excitement. She held the dog close to her, as he continued licking her and letting her know how happy he was with her.

"We've just been calling him Puppy. Or Sweetheart. Or Darling. What'd you have in mind?" the volunteer continued.

"Rick," Alma stated with surety. "I used to watch this show when I was a kid and one of the sidekicks was named Rick and I always thought that if I had a sidekick, I'd want one as cute and loyal and brave as Rick."

Noah stepped closer to her and petted Rick on the head. The dog responded in kind and licked his hand, his tail wagging fiercely against Alma's abdomen.

"Are you ready to sign the paperwork then?" the volunteer asked.

Alma was ready to tell her that she was just dreaming and was in no position to get a dog now, but Noah spoke up and said, "Yeah, let's do it." To Alma, he added, "He can stay with me until you're ready." She glared at him, watching him as he smiled and gazed at her with hope in his eyes.

Forget intervention, he was still trying to convince her to pursue a relationship with him.

Anger at the betrayal, Alma thrust the dog into his arms and walked back to the car. Noah had left the doors unlocked, so she sat inside stewing while she waited for him to follow. What was wrong with him? Didn't he understand what kind of person she was? Didn't he see what she was capable of?

Alma waited but Noah delayed in coming out. She thought about going back inside and telling him she was ready to go just in case he hadn't gotten the hint, but she didn't want him thinking she would chase after him either. That wasn't the way this worked—men chased after her.

Minutes later, Noah emerged from the shelter with Rick in his arms. He walked over to the driver's side of the car and placed the puppy on the seat. The dog immediately jumped into Alma's lap. She tried to ignore him, but his sparkling eyes and wagging tail did her in. She held him as Noah sat down and started the car.

"Take me back," she demanded coldly.

"Nope," Noah remarked. "You still owe me dinner."

"We had dinner."

"That was dessert."

"Take me back or I'll…"

Nothing came to mind though. Noah waited for a moment for her to say something, but when she didn't, he backed out of the parking spot and put the car in drive. He braked long enough to look at her and say, "I'll take you back after dinner," before he drove off.

Seeing that he wasn't going to budge, Alma stopped arguing. She remained quiet for the remainder of the trip while Rick pulled out of her embrace and leaned into the window to look at the passing scenery. Alma watched him with envy. If she could only have a fraction of his curiosity and happiness…

Noah drove her back to his apartment complex. Alma took hold of Rick once again and exited the car. She walked over to Noah who was holding his hand out to her. She considered taking it, remembering the feel of it, but she didn't. She would be leading him on, and she had done enough of that. Instead, she tightened her hold on Rick and waited on Noah to lead her inside, so she could get this dinner over and done with.

He took the hint and together they went inside and back up to the roof. The view was still incredible; every-thing else had changed though. There were new cushions on the chairs, prettier ones, with new monochromatic lights strung up along the edge. The fire pit was lit and glowing with warmth, while dinner was waiting for them on a TV tray between two chairs: two bowls of cereal, a pitcher of milk, a couple of glasses of orange juice and a pint of ice cream.

Alma was confused about the food. She put Rick down on the floor, then pointed to the tray.

"What's with breakfast?" she asked Noah.

"It was on your list," he replied matter-of-factly.

Alma thought back to what she had written. The only food-related item was the coffee drink with extra whipped cream and sprinkles. Then she remembered she had used an old grocery list as a base for her suicide one. Noah was so sincere in his effort to please her, he had purchased everything on her list. The thought endeared him to her even more. She wanted to jump into arms and let him catch her...but she couldn't do that. She sat down on the closest chair next to her and said, "Noah, stop."

"What?"

"Please stop," she repeated, her heart heavy. "This isn't going to work."

Noah sat across from her.

"Look, I know everything between us was unexpected, but you're here and alive and I've been reading about your condition and I can't pretend to know anything about what you're going through, but there's so much stuff left to do in life, more lists to make." He reached into his back pocket and retrieved her list out of his wallet. Alma hesitantly took it, embarrassed by it now. "I just want for you to see that. I want for you to live, to give life a chance."

Alma glanced at this list and saw the first item she wrote:

Kiss Noah

"And give *us* a chance?" she asked.

He looked down at his hands, as if afraid to see her reject him. Alma's heart broke. She wanted to make him understand he deserved better than her, to help him see she wasn't a good match for him, but even she didn't believe it. She wanted to be with him. She wanted to feel the peace she got around him. She wanted the comfort he was offering.

But she also knew she couldn't do that to him. She was no good; and though she had always been loath to talk about her past, it was the only way to make him understand that he needed to leave her be.

"You know, as bad as 'my condition' is, the manic episodes are pretty good," she began, her eyes fixed upon her lap. "You feel like you're invincible, like you're on top of the world. But then the depression follows, and you feel like you could die there. It's a terrible cycle, up and down. The worst part though is during your high, right before your depression hits, when you know it's coming but there's nothing you can do to stop it. I had been down that road enough times to know I didn't want to die there, so I made the decision to go out on top before the depression returned."

She paused and swallowed hard.

"I dated Finn for a few months, the guy at the restaurant? He's a good guy, he really is, and we had fun together. I knew something was wrong with me, but I did nothing. I was afraid they would tell me I was crazy like my mother. Then a year ago, Finn and I got into a fight in the kitchen of his apartment. He called me an emotional bitch, said I was moody and that he couldn't deal with me anymore. I argued and argued and then somehow, I was holding a knife and I stabbed him. I don't remember doing it, I just know that I did, and I remember being shocked that I could hurt Finn like that. So, I cut my arm, hoping I'd hit a vein. I wanted to die."

Alma held out her arm and pulled up the sleeve of the shirt Noah had given her. She revealed her tattoo, but also the scar beneath it. He touched her arm carefully as if he might hurt her.

"A neighbor called 9-1-1. Leta got a lawyer, convinced Finn not to press charges if I got psychiatric help and stayed away from him. I was hospitalized for a few months and was officially diagnosed: bipolar I depression with hypersexuality. I act out my mania by having sex. Kind of like an addiction, but it manifests itself when I'm manic. It's my high. I can't tell you how many people I've slept with. I just…"

Her voice trailed off for a brief moment before she sucked in her breath and continued.

"They put me on medication and made me attend therapy. All this was supposed to help me, but it didn't. The meds were awful, the side effects were worse, and the moods still changed. I gained weight, I was always nauseous, my hair even started falling out. Every time I saw my doctor, he added another pill. I was taking seven pills a day, and nothing fixed it. Then on top of that, my relationship with Leta changed and I was no longer allowed to see my niece. I wasn't Alma anymore; I was this thing, this sickness that no one understood, or cared to understand. Even I don't understand it. That's when I finally stopped taking the medication and decided to kill myself. To say goodbye, make amends and end my life, before the depression set in. That's why I went to see Finn. I shouldn't have, but I only wanted to say I was sorry. Nothing else."

Alma paused, her body spent. To admit so much hurt, psychologically and physically. She ached all over and wanted to cry, but she was tired of crying. She just wanted Noah to react, to run away, to leave her now that he knew the truth about her.

But he did none of those things. Instead, he moved to the edge of his seat and leaned forward. Then he took her into his arms and held her close to his chest. She knew she should fight him, but he felt so good, so strong, so warm. All she could do was let him hold her.

After a while, Alma pulled out of his embrace and sat back.

"This isn't going to work. Noah, I'm a mess."

He guffawed loudly.

"Well, it's not like I'm perfect either," he replied. "I leave the toilet seat up. I chew with my mouth open. And I've been known to kidnap patients and adopt dogs with them, knowing their sister would cut my balls off and feed them to the dog."

Alma laughed. She remembered her sister mentioning 'that poor boy', but she didn't realize they had interacted for an extended amount of time. However long it was, Noah had pegged Leta correctly.

Noah smiled at her.

"I like hearing you laugh," he remarked, as he touched her face.

Alma groaned inwardly: he was still hopeful. She forced herself to get serious.

"Will you still be saying that in a couple of months when you've had enough of my mood swings? When you're the one I've hurt?"

"But you already hurt me," he said. "When you tried to kill yourself in my arms."

Alma turned away from Noah, her face burning with embarrassment: she never considered how he would feel the next morning, she just acted on her impulses.

"No, I didn't mean it like that," he said drawing her attention back to him. "I only meant you've already done your worst. I was devastated when I woke up and saw you lying there in my arms the next morning, believing you had died. But now that we're on the other side of it, there is nothing worse you can do to hurt me, except give up. I won't pretend that I'm not being selfish here: I want you to get better, but I also want to be a part of that process. I don't know why you kissed me, but there was something there and I want to be around to find out what. I want to get to know you, to help you, to encourage you, to help you find reasons to live. And if I'm not reason enough, then I'll respect that, and I'll be your friend and be there for you however you need me. But I'll be honest, I'm really hoping you'll say okay so that we can see each other," he pleaded, his eyes twinkling with optimistic expectation.

Alma was confused. Why didn't he just go away like all the other guys in her life? Why was he different? Didn't he understand who and what she was? Maybe he was actually the crazy one in need of psychiatric help.

Then again, didn't she deserve everything he was offering? Couldn't she accept it, guilt-free?

Sirens broke through the silence and interrupted their conversation. They grew louder with every passing second. Alma knew they were coming for her and Noah, or rather for Noah *because of her*, and when they pulled up to the building, she had her answer: no, she couldn't.

Twenty-Seven

FROM THE TIME HE CONCEIVED his plan, Noah expected it to fail. He rarely experienced moments of inspiration; and when he did, they usually didn't make it past the stage of commencement. That he had made it this far without police intervention was a miracle. But as law enforcement drove up to the building, lights flashing and sirens blaring, Noah could only wonder at how much their timing sucked.

Yes, Alma argued and pushed him away, but she had begun listening and considering his request. He could see it in her eyes. Then the police had to show up, making her withdraw again. She pulled down her sleeve, covering her tattoo and closing herself off to him in determined resignation. As much as Noah wanted to ask her to make a decision, he knew the moment had passed. It was time for her to go back to the hospital, time for him to own up to the consequences of his actions. He knew getting caught was a possibility from the start, but he hoped, given his clean record, they would be lenient with him.

Noah sighed as he rose to his feet.

"I guess it's time to go," he said and

offered Alma his hand. She accepted and stood up, but she didn't make eye contact. Then he collected Rick; and together, the three of them walked to the door. Noah reached for the knob, but without notice, the door suddenly opened. He and Alma were startled to find they were facing two police officers, who in turn were shocked to see them there. With swift movements, the officer in front pulled out his weapon and aimed it at Noah.

"Hands up," he yelled.

Noah let Rick and Alma go and raised his hands above his head. While the first officer kept his gun on him, the second one walked him back to the chairs and turned him around so he could give him a pat down.

"Is this really necessary?" he asked. "I was taking her back."

The policeman ignored him and continued searching him. Noah started to object again, when he heard another woman's voice. It was Leta. He peeked over his shoulder and saw her embracing Alma, a tall, blonde man hovering over them protectively. Noah could only assume this was Leta's husband, which made the situation even more precarious…for him, especially if the man was inclined to defend Alma.

"Oh my God, Alma, are you okay?" Noah heard Leta say. He tried to watch them, but the officer kept turning his head back to him.

"What are you doing here? You said—"

"I know what I said and I'm sorry. It was a mistake. We'll talk about it later okay? Right now, I need to know if you're alright. Did he hurt you?"

"No."

"Are you sure? Did he touch you?"

"God, Leta, no! Stop."

The officer finished his search and sat Noah down on one of the chairs. Taking advantage of the opportunity, he glanced over at Alma, who looked fragile next to her sister. Leta, for her part, looked like a mama bear protecting her young, which was good—Alma needed the support. Noah would have given anything to be standing there with them, but as circumstances went, this was one he was going to have to dig himself out of, especially if he was ever going to win Leta over. Thanksgiving, Christmas and other holidays would be tense otherwise.

Noah noted how positive his mood was. Reality apparently hadn't set in yet.

The first police officer talked to the man who had arrived with Leta. Noah couldn't hear them, but he had an idea what the conversation was about when Alma's sister proclaimed, "Of course, I want to press charges."

"He didn't do anything!" Alma insisted but Leta wouldn't hear it. She was Alma's guardian and determined to see him punished for his indiscretion. Noah's heart sank into his gut: this was not the evening he had envisioned. Dinner, a kiss and then a car ride back to the hospital with his new girlfriend, not jail with kidnapping charges hanging over him.

Noah groaned. He didn't have money for bail or a lawyer. He'd probably spend the night in jail, and at some point the next day (or next week), he'd go before a judge to be arraigned, which meant he could kiss his job good-bye. Bill had given him a second chance, but Noah couldn't imagine the man making another offer.

The positivity began ebbing away.

Alma, Leta and the man were led downstairs, while Noah was handcuffed and advised of his rights. The officer walked him to the door. Then Noah remembered Rick. He promised Alma to care for the dog until she was out of the hospital and he intended to keep that promise. Tonight, though, he would need help.

"My dog," he told the officer and motioned over to the chair he had occupied, where the puppy was hiding. "My neighbor will take him."

Hedy had helped him prepare the roof for dinner and even called the shelter to expedite the process. Noah hated to impose on her even more, but he had no choice. The officer picked up the dog and the three proceeded towards the elevator to drop the dog off with Hedy. When they arrived on the first floor where Hedy's apartment was located, they found all the neighbors were out in the hallway. This was the second time in a week that Noah had been the center of some crisis involving emergency crews or law enforcement; and now he was being escorted out like a criminal.

Reality was finally started to set it.

They arrived at Hedy's apartment: she was already out in the hallway with her father, talking to other tenants who were growing concerned with the safety of the building. She smiled and ran over when she saw him.

Her father didn't look very happy.

"How did it go?" she asked as she took Rick into her arms.

He scowled at her.

"With Alma, I mean," she clarified. "How did it go with her?"

The officer pushed him along before he could answer. Outside, Noah walked down the front steps, the officer's arm hooked in his. He saw Alma and her sister standing over to the side, talking. She was frowning and upset, her gaze turned towards a side street. He thought about everything she shared, and his heart broke again, remembering the sorrow and pain it caused her. He wanted to take her back into his arms again, but with the officer beside him, Noah knew if he tried anything, he'd be the one going to the hospital tonight.

Then again, maybe if he did, he could see Alma again, he could find her at the hospital and visit with her…

Except you still don't know her last name, idiot, Noah chastised. He mentally kicked himself, then remembered Vera did.

So maybe we can chat about it while we're were both looking for new jobs.

He was so distracted with his thoughts he almost missed his name being called. Noah looked around, but he didn't see anyone who wanted his attention more than the police.

Guess I should be glad the FBI wasn't called in, he thought. They were the ones who usually handled kidnappings on TV. Was that always the case? Maybe he would ask one of the officers. Bill probably had a book on the subject.

"Wait!"

The voice was more audible this time. Noah recognized it as Alma's. He stopped walking, as did the policeman escorting him; and turned around in time to see her running towards them. Noah's heartbeat quickened at the prospect of talking to her again.

Alma stopped in front of him and made purposeful eye contact.

"I thought you were cute and unlike anybody else I had been with. That's why I kissed you," she admitted quietly. "I wanted you."

Noah couldn't believe his ears: she thought he was cute. More than that, she wanted him! Her confession silenced the world around them and changed his focus to just him and her.

"And I want you," he assured her.

"But there's no cure for this," she whispered anxiously.

"Then we'll work through it."

"Why? Why would you put yourself through all this when you don't have to?" she asked, edging closer, genuinely confused.

Noah answered her the only way he knew to.

"Because you changed my world," he said. "And now I want to change yours."

She stared intently into his eyes, looking for any sign of doubt or pretense, but there was none to be found.

"Okay," Alma finally said.

Noah's heart leaped. He had hoped for this moment all day, and now that it was here, he felt emboldened. Though his arms were still restrained, he leaned forward and kissed her, her lips soft and sweet. Alma cupped his face and deepened the kiss, opening her mouth for him. But before he could respond in kind, she was jerked away from him.

"Alma!" Leta yelled, pulling her sister back.

Noah groaned at her sudden absence. But even as Leta fussed, accusing him of taking advantage of Alma, he couldn't help but smile. Alma liked him and would stick around to see him.

"I'll come visit," he promised, as the officer resumed walking him to the squad car.

Ignoring her sister, Alma smiled, her attention fixed upon him.

"You'd better," she threatened.

And as the officer helped him in and shut the door, Noah knew everything was going to be okay. Yes, he was headed to jail. He didn't know Alma's last name or what hospital she was going to. And he probably wouldn't have a job come morning. Still, he had Alma and that's all that mattered.

More Information

To read more about mental illness, visit the following websites:

- National Alliance on Mental Illness (NAMI): www.nami.org
- Mental Health: www.mentalhealth.gov
- Substance Abuse and Mental Health Services Administration: www.samhsa.gov

If you or someone you know is struggling with depression, you can text 'Go' to the Crisis Text Line at 741-741. It's free and confidential; and someone is available to talk to you 24/7. Visit their website at www.crisistextline.org for more information. You can also call the National Suicide Prevention Lifeline (800-273-8255) or NAMI (800-950-6264) for support and local referrals.

Read on for the first chapter of

SPEAK TENDERLY TO HER

First Place, Romance
2015 Latino Literacy Books to Movies Award

Isobel has spent her life running from the mistakes of her past, but she is ready to settle down. Unfortunately, second chances aren't easy to come by, especially when you've hurt the person you love the most and Isobel did that four years ago, when she walked out on her husband Tory.

Thanks to the machinations of their pastor though, Isobel finds herself back under the same roof as Tory. The familiarity has her yearning for what used to be, but she knows there's no way he's going to accept the truth of her return, much less love her again. And she's right: when Tory is confronted with all the pain and emotions he thought he'd left behind, he adamantly refuses to forgive her. But as they spend time together, the love he once felt for her begins to surface.

Now, as the two struggle with forgiving and being forgiven, they find that reconciliation is possible, but only if they look beyond what was and deal with the trouble that's followed Isobel back into Tory's arms.

One

"SHE SAID 'THANK YOU'," Janice stated as she approached Dr. Tory Jamison. She was usually stoic in her duties at the pediatric clinic. Not today though—today her eyes were glistening with unshed tears.

"Who did?" he asked.

"Hannah," the nurse replied, referring to the rambunctious toddler who spent as much time at the clinic as the doctors and nurses who treated her.

"So... what?" he said.

"She thanked me for giving her a shot," the nurse exclaimed. "What child does that? She makes me want to cry for hurting her."

"You're getting soft in your old age," he ribbed as she handed him Hannah's chart. The little girl was his final patient of the day, and then he was gone. He had a date to get ready for—a date with the *beautiful* Officer Rebecca Garner. Rebecca had long, blonde hair and baby-blue eyes. She was taller than his five-foot-ten frame, but this didn't bother him at all. She was perfect, and he was looking forward to spending time with her.

Tory walked over to the Hannah's room, knocked, and then entered. Her mother,

Ashley, a young woman in her mid-twenties, was struggling to keep the girl on the examination table and quickly losing the battle. Hannah twisted her body to the side and slid between her mother and the table, landing with an abrupt thud on the hard floor. She swiftly crawled out of her mother's grasp, not realizing Tory was in her path.

"And where are you going?" he asked, dropping the chart on the table and picking her up. She fought his hold on her until she realized who it was, then she squealed and reached into his breast pocket. She dug in deep but came up empty. She frowned, confused—this was where he usually kept the lollipops he offered to his patients at the end of their visit. Instead Tory pulled one out of his pants pocket and held it up.

"Is this what you're looking for?"

She squealed again and grabbed the treat, wasting no time in pulling off the wrapper. Tory set her down with a smile. He viewed at all his patients as *his* kids, but of them, Hannah was his favorite. Ashley brought her in almost a year earlier for a skin infection that wouldn't go away. He diagnosed her with eczema and began treatment to get the illness under control. Some days were better than others, but for the most part she learned to live with the constant itching and irritation.

What impressed Tory the most about Hannah was her spirit; she was a fighter and didn't let anything stop her. Unfortunately, this often resulted in unplanned trips to the emergency room.

Tory turned to her mother and handed her a prescription.

"Let's see how she does with this cream. Call me if you don't see a change."

Ashley offered him a weary smile and said, "Thank you, Dr. Jamison."

He smiled warmly and exited the room.

TORY WHISTLED as he weaved through traffic on his bicycle. He owned a car, but because he lived only a few miles from the clinic, he chose to ride his bike. If he was feeling really ambitious, he could walk to work, but as it was, he was grateful he didn't have to sit in traffic.

He thought about Rebecca. He was on-call at the hospital the night they met. One of his patients had to be transported to the hospital via ambulance and she had accompanied them. He took note of her as she came in with the family, but it was only when the emergency was over, when Rebecca inquired about the patient, that he fully appreciated her features: her beautiful face, hour-glass figure, and a smile that seemed to brighten up whatever room she was in. She could have easily been a swimsuit model, which was reason enough to hesitate when it came to asking her out, but eventually Tory did and now they were going to go on their first date.

Tory turned into his street, still whistling.

You are such a dork, he thought to himself, as he arrived at the apartment complex. He had lived there for the past ten years and though he thought to move several times, he never did. His apartment was big enough for him; he didn't need any more space and it was a plus he didn't have to worry about yard work. Perhaps one day he'd have a reason to move, but until then he was content right where he was.

Tory was getting his mail out of the central mailboxes when he saw *her* sitting on the bench outside his apartment.

Isobel.

He stopped walking, stopped thinking and for a minute, he even stopped breathing. Only his heart continued to beat, hard, as Isobel raised her head and met his gaze. Her light brown eyes seemed to soak in the light around them and shine as the sun itself. Her dark brown hair was short the last time he saw her, but it had grown out, covering her shoulders and falling softly to her back. She had always been petite, but she had gained weight, giving her a full look that enhanced her figure to radiate sensuality.

Oh, what the hell am I thinking? he thought, giving himself a mental kick. She had left him, and here he was thinking how good she looked?

"Tory!"

He broke eye contact with Isobel and turned to the older gentleman approaching him. It was Pastor Martin, his minister, a stocky, solid fellow who spent the first half of his life in the Navy. While traces of his former life slipped into his conversation every once in a while, there was no doubt whom he served now, which worried Tory.

"What's going on?" he asked, bypassing a greeting. Given the fact that Isobel was sitting at his front door after leaving four years earlier, Tory didn't want to waste time patty-caking around the issue.

"Well how's that for a how-do-you-do?" the older man said, placing a hand on Tory's shoulder. "But I appreciate your candor, so I won't beat around the bush. Isobel came to me earlier today needing help. She's been through a lot and just needs a place to stay. We've got her on a waiting list at the mission, but nothing is available now. I'm asking you to take her in, just for a couple of weeks, until a bed opens up."

Tory had been listened as the man spoke but wasn't sure he heard him right.

"You want me to take her in?"

"Yes."

Pastor Martin didn't flinch, neither did he apologize.

Tory shook his head.

"You've got some balls asking me to do that." He should have been more respectful towards the man but considering the hell he had gone through with Isobel, he didn't feel too reverential at the moment.

"So, I've been told," Pastor Martin said, a hint of humor in his voice.

The minister's calm, almost indifferent attitude irritated him.

"I can't believe you, of all people, would ask that of me," Tory said, raising his voice. He didn't care if Isobel heard—in fact, he hoped she did. She didn't deserve his help, and by the look on her face it seemed she knew it too. He noted her body language, her shame-filled disposition, and knew she was close to tears. *Good*, he thought. "You know what she did," he added.

"Yes. She left. You're right. But she's changed. She's not the woman she used to be and given the fact that she is a child of God, like you are, we can't turn our backs on her."

Tory wasn't moved by the minister's induction of God into the conversation. Obviously, the man wished to guilt him into letting her stay, but that wasn't going to happen.

"I can. Find someone else."

Tory started around the pastor, but the older man wouldn't give up. He took hold of Tory's elbow with enough force to stop him. Tory set the kickstand on the bike and turned back to his pastor.

"I said, find someone else," he said with more conviction. "I'm not doing this for her."

"Someone like who, Tory?"

"I don't know, and to be honest, I don't care. She's been gone four years. Ask her. I'm sure there were other men. Maybe one of them will help," he returned with all the anger and resentment that had accumulated in the past few years.

Pastor Martin was unfazed by the remark. He turned his back to Isobel and said, his voice considerably lower, "I know she hurt you when she left..."

Tory opened his mouth to correct him, to tell him that he was over her and didn't want anything to do with the situation, but Pastor Martin held his hand up.

"I'm not excusing what she did. You're a good man, Tory, and these past four years have not been easy. I understand that. But I am coming to you as a man who is responsible for others. I'm not asking you to do this for her, but for me. I'm asking you to help me by helping her. You work at the clinic. You see people every day who are often one day, one paycheck, one wrong decision away from poverty. I see families who are living on the streets, living in their cars, that I have to turn away because I have no room, or I lack the resources. It breaks my heart to do so and if I have a chance to help someone, then I will find a way to do it. Please."

The man wasn't wrong. The clinic, which was located on the hospital campus, provided medical services to low- and no-income patients and families. Including Hannah. Her mom was a single mother who worked overnights to make ends meet, and because that wasn't enough, she had to rely on public assistance to pay for the ever-increasing medical visits that resulted from Hannah's condition and her unstoppable zeal for life. Knowing their situation, Tory determined long ago he would bend over backwards to make sure Ashley and Hannah stayed off the streets. What Pastor Martin was asking of him was no different.

But it was Isobel he was asking for.

You can't turn your back on her..., came the voice in the back of his mind.

She was the one who turned her back on me, he argued back.

Look at her; she's scared. You have to let her stay...

Tory gazed back at Isobel. Her head was hanging low. Her cheeks were flushed, and it was apparent that she was embarrassed. Isobel was finally reaping what she had sowed.

But no one, not even her, deserved to live on the streets.

Dammit, he thought and sighed with disgust. As much as he wanted to walk away, he couldn't just leave her sitting there on the bench.

He shook his head and turned back to Pastor Martin.

"Fine," he muttered.

The older man smiled and clasped his hand on Tory's shoulder. His grip was tight, reminding Tory of the years he spent in the military; even after retiring, the man was still a formidable force. There was no way Tory could have said 'no' to him.

Pastor Martin walked by him to talk to Isobel, who rose as he approached. Tory watched her, unsure of what he was feeling.

Anger? Definitely. Compassion? Hardly.

Fear… Fear? Of what? Isobel leaving again? No, on the contrary, he thanked God this would only be for two weeks.

Tory turned back to his bike. He kicked the stand up and walked it to the front door. Pastor Martin picked up Isobel's bag and placed his arm around her shoulders, almost nudging her forward. Tory unlocked the front door and carried his bike over the threshold into the foyer where he parked it. He walked into the small kitchen, dropped his bag on the counter, and turned around to face them.

Isobel quietly took a few steps into the kitchen with Pastor Martin behind her. He walked past her and offered Tory his hand.

"Thank you, Tory," he said sincerely.

"Two weeks, right?" Tory asked as he took the man's hand.

"That's all. I'll call you and keep you updated," he returned.

Tory acknowledged him and escorted him to the door. Pastor Martin thanked him again and left.

Only when he latched the door did the reality of the situation set it. He was alone with Isobel. For two weeks. Tory took a deep breath and turned around.

Isobel remained where she stopped in the kitchen, her gaze set on the floor. She seemed humbler, quieter, and dejected—hardly the woman he once knew. She had changed for sure.

Tory cleared his throat.

"You know where everything is," he muttered, and started around Isobel. She backed up as he came close to her, like she was afraid of him. He rolled his eyes and brushed past her quickly.

Tory was halfway to his bedroom when he heard her call his name. He stopped walking but didn't turn around.

"I'm...sorry," she said softly. "I didn't want to come here...I mean, after everything that happened...I'm sorry."

Tory shook his head and continued walking. He slammed the door to his room and leaned back against the wall, inhaling deeply. This was a bad idea, a very bad idea. If he had to be around her for two weeks while she dredged up the past, he was going to lose his mind. He would just have to stay gone, starting with tonight.

Without another thought, Tory grabbed a fresh change of clothes and went back out into the hallway to the bathroom. Tory quickly showered up, dressed, grabbed his keys and wallet, and left. He didn't see Isobel, so he assumed she had already made herself at home in the spare bedroom. Hopefully she'd stay there.

He drove around for a while before settling on a pub downtown that he frequented when he was out with friends. Tonight though, it was just him and he was glad—he didn't want to justify his decision to anyone.

Acknowledgements

A big thank you to my family, my editor, my beta readers and all the folks who continue to believe in me. This book and all the others I've written would not have come to life without your love, your support and your assistance. And for that I am grateful.

About the Author

Ruth E. Griffin could draw pictures before she could put sentences together. Eventually, though, she figured out how to do both and is now the author of several books (fiction and non-fiction) which center on women's experiences. She still designs but focuses all her free time on writing. Ruth currently lives in North Carolina with her husband and three children. Her work is available at major online bookstores, while new book release and event information can be found at www.ruthegriffin.com. Email her at ruthegriffin@outlook.com.